La₁ had
gone. ₁ she
had felt then. Abandoned. Humiliated. Foolish.

Now, in the revealing morning light, she was happy to replace those uncomfortable feelings with anger and dislike. She knew why he had been in such a hurry to get away from her. He'd belatedly remembered what was waiting for him back at his villa. A wife and baby!

The Author

Andrea Fuller's meeting with her husband was a fairytale holiday romance. Over twenty years and four children later, she says the romance has never ended. She lives in Brisbane, Australia and is passionate about all it has to offer. She also loves reading, crosswords, yoga, hiking and eating out. She is a qualified accountant, but these days, prefers playing with words rather than numbers.

For my husband, Ken
My hero

Andrea Fuller

Heart's Desire

Published in the USA in 2006

SALTWATER PRESS
P.O. Box 535, Merrylands NSW 2160
AUSTRALIA

www.rockyriverromance.com

ISBN
1-74062-025-9

One

"DIDN'T your mother teach you how to dress properly?"

As soon as the words left Rick's mouth, he regretted them. But none of the dismay churning in his stomach showed on his face. He unconsciously straightened his dark blue tie and continued to lean nonchalantly against the bar at Butterfly Bay Resort on St John Island. While he inwardly cringed at his incredible rudeness, outwardly he was a picture of cool confidence.

The woman stilled. She remained poised on the edge of the barstool, a tableau of frozen disbelief. Finally, she tossed a handful of her glorious, honey blonde hair over one shoulder and slowly turned to face him. She pinned him with cold eyes.

Rick swallowed. He resisted the temptation to apologize... and the urge to straighten his tie again. He was in the right, after all. Unfortunately, he couldn't prevent his eyes flicking down to her cleavage. Luscious, well-rounded breasts threatened to burst from the tiny, skin-tight tee shirt that barely skimmed her midriff. Her hips, and not much else, were covered in a brightly patterned, ultra-short sarong. Her feet were bare.

The woman narrowed her emerald-green eyes and tightened her hand around the frosty glass she had just picked up. For one horror-filled second, Rick was sure she would toss the contents in his face, but she apparently thought better of it.

Instead, she looked straight into his eyes and took a deliberate sip of the tall, blue cocktail. Rick watched, mesmerized, as she slid the tip of her tongue over her top lip. His mouth dried as he imagined his own tongue tracing each of her full, soft lips before his mouth finally plundered hers.

"Didn't your mother ever teach you manners?" she purred, her voice husky and provocative.

Rick tried desperately to be disgusted by her deliberate come-on, but as his groin tightened, he could only be disgusted with himself. She epitomized everything he distrusted in the female species. She was obviously very aware of the effect her body had on men and had no qualms about using it.

He, on the other hand, prided himself on the discipline he had over his baser instincts. He had no intrinsic need for sex. In the appropriate relationship he could enjoy it, but it held no appeal for its own sake. No woman had ever caused him to question the moral principles drummed into him from an early age... until now.

He didn't like it one bit.

"As it happens, yes, but where my mother came from, women dress like ladies," he managed stiffly.

This was going from bad to worse! It was one thing to think she was lacking in basic propriety, but quite another to voice it. What was it about this woman that forced him to blurt out opinions better kept to himself?

He had been watching her all night as she flagrantly downed one drink after another, while flaunting herself at the vacationers who used the island as an overnight anchorage for their yachts.

From his vantage point at the bar, he had been fascinated by the way the flickering light from the open fire was reflected in her glossy hair. Her infectious laugh and the way she threw her head back in delight, exposing a long sinuous neck, had made him swallow. Hard.

When she had left her seat, casually uncurling her bare legs from under her, then headed straight for him, he had almost panicked. She had ignored him. Instead, she caught the barman's eye and ordered yet another drink for herself. Perversely, he had felt let down.

The unwanted attraction must have scrambled his brain. Or was it another part of his anatomy that was causing him to act so out of character? He had been accused of being cold and unresponsive in the past and part of him had believed that cruel remark. Now, he wasn't so sure...

The woman dropped the coy, flirtatious manner. "It's a shame your mother didn't bring up her son to be a gentleman. Now, if you'll excuse me?"

"Wait!"

She turned back again, and he was momentarily distracted by a waft of her musky scent. Any words that may have been forming in his head were gone like a gust of wind. She was gorgeous.

She gave him a glacial stare.

"Well?" she snapped. "Any more insults you'd like to bestow on me?"

"Look. I'm sorry. I had no right..."

"You said it."

"Can I buy you a drink? To apologize."

The hostility changed to consternation. "A drink?" she asked slowly. She appeared perplexed, but not half as shocked as he was at his own words.

He felt his face grow hot and it made him angry. "Yes, a drink. We could talk."

"Oh?" Her eyes widened. She didn't look as sure of herself as she had a minute ago.

"Perhaps we could go down to the beach. Just a walk," he added hurriedly. He felt like a fool and wondered whether it would be easier to cut and run.

The expression on her face was unreadable. "Okay." She smiled. "And, by the way, my name is Lauren." She raked her wickedly sexy eyes over his body before meeting his eyes in a challenging stare.

Rick's stomach dropped. *Now I've really done it.*

For the first time in his life, Rick wished the proverbial floor would open up and swallow him. He dismissed the temptation to announce that he had made a mistake and race back to his villa. Instead, he tried to figure out whether his brain had shut down completely or was just out to lunch.

"I'll have a Blue Lagoon," the woman said sweetly when, after several tension-filled seconds, he still hadn't made any move to ask what drink she would like.

He raised his eyebrows. "A what?"

She was staring at him with those amazing eyes again. The coldness had disappeared. She grinned and held up her empty glass. "A Blue Lagoon. It's delicious. You should try it."

He suspected she was laughing at him and grimaced. "I think I'll pass," he mumbled before turning to the barman.

"A Blue...er, Lagoon for the lady, thanks. And I'll have a Scotch on ice." Hell, he would need a double – make that a triple – at the rate he was going. What was he going to say to this woman? Maybe he should get out more?

The barman placed the drinks in front of them. Rick was grateful for something to do as he lifted his glass and took a healthy swig of straight spirit.

"You still haven't told me your name," Lauren pointed out. She had a genuine, open smile he realized as his nervousness threatened to swamp him. If his senior staff back at Corinella Aged Care Services could see him now, they wouldn't recognize him. Or worse, his reputation as a hard-nosed player in the industry would be shot.

"I'm Rick," he said gruffly. "Rick Masters."

They each sipped their drinks silently for a few minutes while Rick searched his confused brain for a safe topic of conversation. What did one talk about with a woman like her? What on earth could they possibly have in common?

Lauren put her half-finished drink firmly down onto the bar and stood up. She stared into his face expectantly.

He cast another quick glance over her half-naked, but definitely delectable, body. What a fool he must look in his sports jacket and knife-pleated trousers.

"Well, Rick, can you come up with the goods?"

"I beg your pardon!"

She grinned. "Are we going for that walk, or not?"

Lauren woke, heart pounding, to the sound of a baby crying. She sat up and swept a shaking hand through her sweat-damp hair.

For a moment she wasn't sure where she was. She glanced around the airy Haitian-style villa then expelled the air in her lungs in a whoosh. The natural timber walls, high, thatched ceiling and a scattering of her own belongings around the room were familiar. She was safe in her villa on the island of St. John in the Caribbean, where she had been vacationing for the past week.

She dismissed the sound that had woken her as seagulls. Then she heard the plaintive whimper of the baby again and knew she had been right the first time. That was no gull. Her blood ran cold.

She threw back the sheet that had been her only covering during the balmy, late-summer night and flew to the kitchenette. The nerve-jarring sound continued while she groped blindly for the cold-water tap. She splashed water on her flushed cheeks and gulped mouthfuls of it.

She desperately needed to escape, but logical thought processes had ceased functioning. Her confused brain couldn't sift through the maelstrom of images to figure out what to do next.

The baby's pitiful howls stopped abruptly, but it was too late. Lauren's nerves were shattered. She could still hear the cries in her head, cries that were gut-wrenchingly similar to those of her nightmares.

She ran to the tiny bathroom, leaned into the shower stall and twisted the tap with unnecessary violence. She stared at herself in the bathroom mirror. Her hair looked like a haystack, even taking into account her preference of late for a ruffled, unruly style. Her eyes looked huge in their mascara-smudged sockets. Even her lips seemed bruised. She was a mess.

Unwanted recollections of the previous evening taunted her. A frown of disapproval. An engaging smile. Strong, protective arms. Right at that moment, she couldn't put a name to the disturbing memories. But she was grateful he could not see her now.

Last night she had been too tired to remove her make-up and brush out her wild curls before she had gone to bed. Too drunk, a sneaky voice in her brain corrected her.

"I was not drunk," she snapped, as if someone had actually spoken. "Just a bit tipsy," she added airily.

Lauren looked down at herself, ignored the fullness of her breasts and squeezed her eyes shut when her glance reached her bare stomach. She groaned as she stepped into the shower stall and snapped the sliding door closed. For the first time since waking, she realized she had a thumping headache.

"I was not drunk," she repeated to herself. "And, besides, that's what vacations are for – to have a good time."

She didn't voice the rest of the words tugging at the edge of her thoughts. A few drinks helped to forget the trauma of the last few months. Months when her rosy future had been snatched from her. Months when she had feared she would never be happy again.

Following on from the realization of her headache were rumblings of nausea, which may have been part of a hangover or merely hunger. She chose to believe the latter as she quickly washed her hair and dressed in the first thing that came to hand; a short, cotton dress with shoe-string straps in a striking crimson and white batik print.

She dragged a brush through her damp curls and fluffed them up with her fingers. As she did so, she breathed deeply from the warm breeze wafting through the open wooden louvers. Relieved that she had her fickle emotions under control, she slipped her feet into sandals and left the villa.

As Lauren hurried down the steps from the porch, she glanced sideways toward her neighbor. She gasped, arrested by the scene before her. So great was her shock, that she almost missed her footing on the bottom step. Lying asleep in a hammock hanging from the villa's porch was the man she had encountered the previous evening.

His dark hair, so smooth and tamed last night, was now a mop of thick waves falling carelessly over his forehead. Lauren gulped as her eyes slid over the curling matt of hair on his chest and the dark shadow on his angular, unshaven jaw. Nestled into the crook of his arm, like a sleeping cherubic angel, lay a baby.

Lauren stood frozen, trying to grasp what her eyes were telling her. In an instant, shock changed to fury. A boiling anger at the man's obvious deception threatened to erupt.

Just in time, she stopped herself from marching over to him and shoving him out of the hammock. It was the baby that stopped her, whether from fear of harming it or fear of the baby itself, Lauren had no intention of considering. Besides, she wouldn't deliberately upset his trusting wife, who was no doubt inside the villa.

The nausea that had, up until then, been only an unpleasant sensation, suddenly became an urgent need to throw up. She took a deep, calming breath. When her stomach settled again, she bolted down the gravel pathway to the buffet breakfast laid out in the restaurant. Putting food and caffeine, not necessarily in that order, into her churning stomach, suddenly became a top priority.

After a cup of strong coffee, Lauren felt marginally human again. She helped herself to a plate of freshly cut tropical fruit, re-filled her cup and took her breakfast to a table in the far corner of the restaurant veranda.

She savored the refreshing sweetness of pineapple, mango and nashi fruit, and basked in the muted morning sunshine. Gradually, the tension evaporated from her body. She licked the sticky, sweet juice from her fingers and leaned back into the soft canvas of her chair. She stared dreamily out through the lightly swaying coconut palms to the beach and turquoise ocean beyond. She tried to blank out everything that had happened during the last twelve hours.

The same three yachts that had arrived yesterday were bobbing in the gentle swell of the lagoon. Lauren could just make out two of the men she had been laughing and chatting with the night before. They were standing on the deck of one of the boats, talking, while consulting a map and pointing across the inlet. As she watched, a woman came up on deck, followed closely by another. Each man hugged and kissed the women and it was at that point that Lauren turned away.

It shouldn't have bothered her – seeing people she had only just met so content – but it did. And it was all his fault. Her vacation and recovery from post-traumatic stress had been going so well until that man had come along.

Yes, she had flirted with the yachtsmen as they all relaxed after dinner, but even the women had found it harmless fun. Not like Mr. Wet Blanket. He had spent the whole time glaring at her from across the room. And the more she had sensed his disapproval, the more outrageous her behavior had become.

Rick Masters. That was his name, Lauren remembered now. Actually, Richard suited him better. Richard the Stuffed Shirt. Everything about him had screamed conservatism – from his short, perfectly groomed hair, to his immaculate sports jacket and his spit-polished leather lace-ups. He had even been wearing a tie – on an island resort, for heaven's sake! But then, he had not been such a stuffed shirt later in the evening.

A lop-sided smile tugged at her mouth. No, Rick had not been so formal by the time she had finished with him.

The smile slid away. She had let her natural friendliness go a bit overboard, and it was not something she wanted to dwell on. The exact details were something of a blur, but the snippets that were crystal clear made her cringe with embarrassment.

Despite her sense of fun and tendency to chat with just about anyone, she was not normally so loose with her affections. But Rick had pushed her to the limit. She had been able to sense every disapproving lecture her father had ever delivered, oozing from the man's supercilious pores.

How dared he judge her and try to control her behavior as her father always had! But he wasn't her father. She couldn't for the life of her figure out why she had allowed him to get under her skin.

Accepting a drink from him had been her first mistake, she reflected now. Going for a moonlight stroll along the beach had been her second.

The third and fatal mistake had been the kiss.

She groaned, letting her head fall into her hands, mortified as the memory cleared. It had hardly been more than a peck and his look of offended surprise had been amusing at the time. It had also been the perfect opening for him to insult her. Again...

"Didn't your mother teach you not to kiss a man until you were invited?" he had drawled even as Lauren had wondered if her sense of fun had taken her too far.

To overcome her embarrassment, she hit back at his patronizing tone. "Yes, but she also told me that if I kissed a toad, he'd turn into a prince. I decided to try it out." Her lips were still tingling from the playful brush with his mouth and she pushed aside the fact that he was definitely not a toad.

"And?"

Lauren shrugged with feigned indifference. "It seems mothers don't know everything."

She thought she saw something like hurt in Rick's face for a fleeting moment, but she must have been mistaken. His jaw tightened and his lips thinned.

"Your mother has a lot to answer for," he said.

She gave him a knowing smile. "Perhaps we could try again. My assessment of your ability may have been a little hasty."

He looked affronted and opened his mouth to speak. Before he could voice what was bound to be another put-down, Lauren leaned across and captured his mouth.

She had meant it to be another teasing, flirtatious attempt to antagonize him, but almost from the first touch, her daring intentions lost their appeal.

His lips were soft and seductive, his mouth hot and inviting. She felt him give in to the kiss in the same instant she relaxed into his body. His arms came around her as she smoothed her hands under his jacket and over his hard, muscled back. Somewhere in the back of her mind a thought fluttered that his athletic body was at odds with his old-fashioned exterior. The thought floated away before she could pin it down.

She bit back a whimper as a delicious excitement stormed through her body, every sensation clamoring for attention. The blood in her veins throbbed with anticipation, a burgeoning desire in the pit of her stomach threatened to overwhelm.

But, most of all, it felt good to be held against a strong, male body. She felt comforted. Protected. It was a feeling she had craved in all those lonely weeks since Brian had jilted her.

But Brian had never made her feel like this!

The realization startled her. It also made her question her judgment. And her sanity.

A dozen unpleasant thoughts trampled the wondrous feelings assailing her body, but she refused to let them take hold. She was in no hurry to relinquish the wonderful feeling of being in Rick's arms. It should have mattered that he was a perfect stranger, but somehow, he just didn't feel like one. Her body responded to him like a long lost lover.

She felt the heat of him through his clothes, against her bare skin. His hardness. His gentleness. The strength of him.

Suddenly, Rick pushed her away. "Maybe we should take a break?"

For a split second Lauren was mortified, but she shoved her embarrassment aside.

"Spoil sport," she pouted, pleased that her voice didn't tremble. "Why did you ask me down here, if it wasn't for a bit of fun?"

He looked horrified but then his eyes narrowed. "As it happens, I thought you might have underestimated the trouble you could get into with those men. I believed my intervention was called for."

Lauren laughed with genuine amusement. When she saw the stern expression on Rick's face, she stopped. "You're serious!" Not even Brian had been that sanctimonious.

"Of course. It's not a joking matter."

She linked her arms loosely around his neck and looked soulfully into his eyes, trying for a seductive pout. She had to avoid the danger of taking the feelings he could evoke seriously. "So why did you rescue me? Do you want me for yourself?"

He firmly removed her arms from his neck. "No. I just didn't want to see you make a fool of yourself or get out of your depth."

"What's that supposed to mean? Who made you my keeper? You don't even know me. And... and you sound like my father."

"You were deliberately leading those guys on. I doubt whether they would have taken 'no' for an answer if you'd changed your mind."

"That's ridiculous! Their wives were there."

"Even so, they may have laid in wait for you later. I just didn't want it on my conscience if something happened to you."

Lauren wondered how she could possibly be attracted to such pompous arrogance. "How touching, but I can assure you, I can look after myself. I am twenty-five."

"Age has nothing to do with common sense."

Lauren felt her blood pressure rising. She wanted to walk away, yet something stopped her. "I'm quite adept at handling myself," she snapped.

"Then why are you on a deserted beach with a total stranger. I could be straight off 'America's Most Wanted' for all you know. Or are you used to being alone with strange men?"

Lauren ignored the pointed slur and scoffed instead. "I happen to be a very good judge of character. I knew the moment I clapped eyes on you, you were so proper even a naked woman would be safe." She laughed at the offended expression on his face.

Suddenly her legs were whipped out from under her and she landed with a thud on the sand, flat on her back. Her arms were pinned above her head, a heavy weight pressed onto her chest.

"Are you absolutely sure about that?" Rick growled.

She squirmed and kicked, but the struggle was useless. He lay like a dead weight over her body.

"Get off me, you... you... animal," she squeaked in frustration.

Immediately, she was released. She got up gracelessly, brushing the sand from her legs and tugging the hem of her sarong.

"What was that all about?" She watched him from under lowered eyes as she backed away.

He didn't smile. "Just teaching you a lesson."

"I'm going back now. You've spoiled my evening."

Why had everything gone terribly wrong? All week, she'd successfully blanked out the real world waiting for her back in Miami, now he had spoiled it. She remembered how she had felt the moment she'd seen Rick walk into the restaurant before dinner. Her heartbeat had gone into overdrive. When he had later bought her a drink and invited her for a walk, she had told herself to enjoy the moment. Now the bubble had gone out of the cocktails, leaving her feeling flat and fuzzyheaded.

"I haven't spoiled anything. You managed that by yourself. You should never flirt unless you're prepared for the consequences," Rick said sternly.

"Rubbish! What Victorian novel did you escape from?"

"There's nothing wrong with decent behavior."

Is he for real? She took a step closer to him, clasped her fingers loosely behind his neck and lifted her face to his. "Oh, loosen up, Grandpa," she murmured seductively against his mouth before sliding her tongue gently across his bottom lip. When she got no immediate reaction, she kissed his closed mouth.

He stiffened, but when she wrapped her arms around him and sighed, "Kiss me", his mouth relaxed and he gathered her close.

It gave her a heady feeling of power, to say nothing of the delicious tingles fizzing through her body. Without debating the merits of exploring further, she tentatively slipped her tongue between his lips. It felt unbelievably good to be held against his hard body again and she immediately forgot her play-acting. His mouth melted into hers as if they were meant to be together. She should have been feeling nervous at taking the initiative. Instead, she knew she was safe with him. The cold feeling of loneliness that had threatened a few moments before flew away on the ocean breeze.

The warm sand squeezed between her toes and she could hear the swishing of tiny waves as they rippled onto the shore. Her problems, and the rest of the world faded into insignificance.

His fingers were warm and firm against her bare waist. Impatient for more, she guided his hand upwards and sighed as his fingertips became a firebrand skimming along the underside of her bra-less breasts.

She waited, anticipating the moment when he would find her burgeoning nipples. She silently begged him to rub the palms of his hand over them, to squeeze them lightly before lowering his head and suckling each one in turn.

Rick abruptly released her. Lauren stepped back, bewildered. She stared into his bemused eyes trying to read his mind. He had wanted her as much as she had wanted him. She knew it. She also knew he hated himself for it. It was written all over his face.

The confusion in his eyes cleared and he lifted his arm to look at his watch. "Good heavens, is that the time? I almost forgot. I've got to go."

Lauren was stunned. As an insult, it was more effective than his previous cutting observations.

"Don't let me keep you," she bit out with as much sarcasm as she could muster.

He looked at her and frowned. "I... I'm sorry about what just happened. I don't know what... I'm sorry. I have to go. There's something I need to take care of."

He looked flustered. Actually, he looked as if he couldn't get away from her fast enough, Lauren reflected bitterly. She snapped, "Forget it. I suddenly feel tired myself."

"Would you like me to walk you back to your villa?" He didn't sound thrilled with the idea.

"No, I'll be fine. Don't let me keep you," she repeated scornfully in an attempt to hide the tremble in her voice.

"Right. Well. Goodnight, then. I guess I'll see you tomorrow."

She nodded as he turned and disappeared into the night.

Lauren had remained on the beach long after he had gone. Unfortunately, she remembered clearly the way she had felt. Abandoned. Humiliated. Foolish.

Now, in the revealing morning light, she was happy to replace those uncomfortable feelings with anger and dislike. She knew why he had been in such a hurry to get away from her. He'd belatedly remembered what was waiting for him back at his villa. A wife and baby.

She leaned back in the canvas chair and stared at the ocean, sullenly reflecting on the many and varied faults of men in general.

"May I join you?"

Lauren's head swung around and the steady beat of her heart tripped to a halt before resuming at a faster pace.

"Oh, it's you." She made no attempt at civility. The smoothly tamed hairstyle was back in place but she could see a tantalizing hint of dark curls at the V of his pale blue shirt. She was tempted to ask where he'd lost his tie.

Rick frowned. "I see you're feeling the effects of last night. Not so lively this morning?"

"Don't you have to be somewhere?" She didn't know whether anger or embarrassment was uppermost in her mind.

He glanced at his watch. "Not for another hour or so." He picked up her empty coffee cup. "Can I get you a refill?"

"No thanks, I was just leaving."

"Not on my account, I hope."

"As a matter of fact, yes."

He put the cup back down. "I see."

Lauren stood up, and then regretted the sudden movement when her head started pounding. She was tempted to drop back into her seat; instead she pushed past Rick when he made no effort to move out of her way.

"See you later," Rick called after her.

"Not if I see you first," Lauren muttered.

Rick closed the space between them and detained her with a firm touch on her arm. "Have I offended you?" he asked softly. "If I have, I'm sorry. I regret what happened last night. I was way out of line and –"

She spun around. "I don't know what game you're playing at, but I might as well tell you right now, I'm in the villa next to yours."

He looked puzzled. "And?"

"Don't act dumb. I might have been a pushover last night, but you can't keep your secret from me any longer." She shook his hand off and glared at him, her hands on her hips. "I was awake earlier than planned this morning and it wasn't the sweet trill of birds that woke me – if you get my drift."

His face cleared. "I'm sorry, did Melanie disturb you?"

More than you could know. "So you admit you have a baby now, do you?"

"It's not what you –"

"You lied to me!" Lauren couldn't hide the anguish from her voice.

Rick looked bewildered. "I did?"

"Don't try to deny it – you lied by omission."

"What are you talking about?"

"You have a baby."

"Yes, Melanie is staying with me, but –"

"I suppose you have some sort of open marriage."

"I'm not married."

"And that makes it all right?" she scoffed.

"Makes what all right?"

She nearly stamped her foot in frustration. "You have a baby and a... girlfriend, or whatever she is, and you let me believe you were available."

He smiled disarmingly and she got a sudden glimpse of a different Rick. "Are you interested?" he asked softly.

"Don't change the subject," she snapped, angry with herself for being affected by the warmth in his smile, the way it gave his stern face a distinctly playful look. How dare he flirt with her! Especially after all that judgmental rubbish he had spouted last night.

His smile faded and she was surprised to see him blush. He pushed his fingers through his hair. "I do not have a wife, fiancée, lover or even a geisha girl. I arrived at the island late yesterday, alone and without the questionable advantage of female company, unless you count Melanie, and she's only six months old." He held up his hand when she went to cut him off again. "If you would give me a chance to explain! Melanie is my sister's baby. I'm baby sitting."

Lauren's shoulders sagged. "Oh."

"Yes, 'oh'."

"I guess I should offer my apology."

"Only if you want to."

"It's your own fault. You still should have told me about the baby."

"Would you believe, you distracted me so much, I nearly forgot about Melanie altogether?"

Lauren chose to ignore that. "So, who's minding her now?"

"Cathy, one of the waitresses. I'm in a bit of a spot, actually. I was supposed to be leaving Melanie with my other sister, Janice, and her husband, Carl, but –"

"Forget it. I don't want to hear your life story."

"That's okay, then." He looked hurt, but Lauren couldn't afford to be sentimental. Just because Melanie wasn't his baby and just because he appeared to be unattached after all, didn't mean she should suddenly forget her own circumstances. She could feel her pulse rate accelerating and her breath catching at the mere thought of babies.

"Look, I really have to go," she said quickly, the insidious creep of panic edging along her veins. "I have something urgent to attend to."

"On an island resort?" Rick asked in disbelief.

She backed away. "Yes!"

He snagged her arm as she turned to go, but she refused to face him. She cursed the stupid tears stinging the back of her eyes, blinking furiously. She didn't even know why she felt like crying. Even if she could forget the baby, the guy wasn't worth crying over. He was arrogant, impossibly old-fashioned, judgmental and out of touch with reality.

She took a deep breath and looked meaningfully at the large, firm hand still holding her elbow.

"If you don't mind..."

He released her. "Sorry, but I seem to have upset you again. I'd like to make it up to –"

She pinned a vacuous smile on her face and cut him off. "Don't worry about me, Rick, darling. Nothing you could say would upset me."

She turned and walked rapidly away before he could further detain her... and before she really did burst into tears.

Rick sat in the chair that Lauren had just vacated. He stared at her empty coffee cup. After the recent upheavals and grief in his life, the last thing he felt equipped to deal with was another complication. And there was no doubting that Lauren was just that.

He still couldn't fully comprehend how his feelings had gotten out of control to such an extent last night. For someone who had never had a problem controlling his feelings, the immediate, overwhelming attraction he felt for Lauren was unnerving to say the least.

What threw him the most was that she wasn't even his type. She was flighty, full of beans and seemed determined to take life as casually as possible – perhaps a little too determined, he reflected now. While she projected an image of being out for nothing more than a good time, he still couldn't help feeling her actions didn't quite ring true.

In a matter of hours he had gone from being a confirmed bachelor with a sure knowledge of what he wanted from life, to a man longing for an elusive something he couldn't quite put his finger on.

Two

LAUREN'S headache did not improve as the morning wore on. Memories and emotions that she had recently congratulated herself for having firmly under control, poked and prodded at her psyche with unnerving persistence. And it didn't take a genius to figure out why. Those feelings, only precariously controlled, she now realized, seemed to respond to something in Rick.

She found herself a shady spot away from the main part of the beach. It was a peaceful patch of sand and she dragged one of the sun lounges up to the shade of a coconut palm. The tranquil waters of the lagoon lapped at the powdery white sand only a few feet away.

The tranquility failed to pervade Lauren's unsettled mind. The thick book she had brought with her hadn't held her attention, despite the fact she had reluctantly put it down the day before at a particularly suspenseful stage in the plot.

She found herself thinking about Rick. She berated herself for the weakness of her thoughts, but the daydreams persisted. The image of the baby snuggled into him taunted her. That fleeting glimpse had torn at her heart. Never mind that she had only just met him. Try telling her instincts that.

She shrugged and tried to dismiss the useless yearning. What did it matter, when there was no point in anything but a passing relationship? Brian had made sure of that.

She was determined to regain her equilibrium, refusing absolutely to succumb to the horror of the panic attacks she endured after the procedure and Brian's perfidy. She had been fully recovered, until Rick had come onto the scene. She wouldn't let him undermine that recovery by allowing him to sit in judgment of her.

The simple solution was to steer clear of him. And the baby. Even on an island this size, how hard could that be? She picked up the book again, determined to get back into the escapism of Ruth Rendell's latest mystery.

"Hi. I don't think you've met Melanie." Rick's voice sliced through Lauren's tenuous hold on her peace of mind.

She stilled, but her heart surged in her chest. It was a few seconds before she could calm it enough to think clearly. Staring at the book, she mentally readied herself for the inevitable. The print swam before her eyes.

She lifted her head. Her eyes slid to where the baby rested on Rick's hip. Her heart shifted at the captivating image they presented; Father and daughter. Except that they weren't father and daughter, she reminded herself.

Involuntarily, her gaze moved upwards. The baby was chewing on Rick's collar. She seemed to sense Lauren's eyes on her. She stopped and gave Lauren a huge grin.

Lauren forgot where she was. Forgot her pain. Even forgot the man. Her eyes softened and she returned the baby's smile.

"I think she likes you," drawled Rick.

Lauren snapped back to reality. "You're mistaken. I have a complete disinterest in babies. I intensely dislike anything to do with them. In fact, I haven't got a maternal bone in my body." She nearly choked on the horrendous lie.

"I was referring to Melanie," he said quietly. "She likes you, even if you don't like her."

Lauren tried to regroup. "It's nothing personal. I just have this aversion to children of any age."

"I heard you the first time and I didn't believe you the second time either."

Lauren finally looked into Rick's face, and then wished she hadn't. Expecting to find censure, all she saw was sympathy.

She frantically dredged together her shattered control. "Look, it's quite simple. Children cramp my style. Now, if you'll excuse me, I'm sure there are still some unencumbered males left on the island. I have three days to go of my vacation and I aim to enjoy them."

She turned away. She knew she sounded appallingly rude. But if that's what it took to get through to him, so be it. She had made a mistake last night and she had to make every effort to redress it. She blushed when she remembered how her actions could have been construed, *had* been construed by Rick. She had to make it clear that she wanted nothing to do with him.

She stared at the ocean, willing her rampant emotions into a semblance of order. The sea was as flat as plate glass, the sun glinting like diamonds on the surface. She knew Rick was still there. She could feel his presence beside her. After a few seconds of silence she casually turned and looked up. Her eyes slid involuntarily to the glimpse of dark hair at the deep V of his open shirt.

"You still here?" she asked with a less than steady voice.

"There's no need to be rude. I thought I'd keep you company while we're waiting for the lunch bell."

Lauren felt like an absolute heel, but she refused to soften. If she gave her tightly controlled emotions a single inch she'd live to regret it. She just knew he was bad news but she couldn't bring herself to tell him to get lost.

"Please yourself. It's a free country," she eventually managed, with bad grace.

He hunkered down. "Actually, I came to see whether you'd like to sit with me at lunch. I... er, feel we got off to rather a bad start. We could talk..."

Lauren was deeply aware of the attractive rumble of his voice and was equally aware she was in imminent danger of falling under his seductive spell. She had to banish the erotic fantasies invading her subconscious. Now.

She took a deep breath, hating what she had to do to keep her sanity — and her heart — intact. "Rick, darling," she simpered. "You seem to be reading more into our association than you should. I'm afraid I don't have the time or the inclination for deep and meaningful conversations with you. And, if it's the kind of chat we had last night that you're after, well... let's just say, I'm more... um, myself today."

His reaction was almost comical as his face changed from sympathy to dismay. Lauren ploughed on regardless. "I admit, I was a teeny bit annoyed with you this morning, but that was only because I thought you had intended cheating on your wife. I think we should just forget the whole unfortunate misunderstanding. Friends?"

Lauren held out her hand and smiled in what she hoped would be interpreted as carefree equanimity. Meanwhile, her heart lay crushed under a weight of her own making.

Rick stared at her hand for several seconds before finally sliding his palm against hers. "If that's what you want," he said uncertainly.

"It is," she said as she turned back to her murder mystery.

"Interesting book?"

"Oh, yes..." She didn't take her eyes off the page.

"It must be, you're reading it upside down."

Lauren started to turn the book around then stopped. The book was already the right way up.

"Cute, very cute." She snapped the book shut. "Now, if you'll excuse me, I think I'll get ready for lunch." She stood quickly and snatched up her towel and tube of sunscreen, intending to escape to the relative safety of her villa. Wildly, she wondered if there was a cruise that she could book for the next day. Anything to get as far away from Rick and the baby as possible.

She had taken only a few steps up the beach when Rick called her. "Lauren! You forgot something."

With extreme reluctance she stopped and turned. He was holding her book in his hand.

"Rats," she muttered under her breath.

He strode over and held out the book. She plastered a plastic smile on her face and plucked it from his hand. "Thanks a lot," she said as she turned away again.

Rick grabbed Lauren's arm, preventing her escape. The woman was driving him crazy, but he had no intention of letting her call all the shots. She had overplayed her hand. That ridiculous act back there was so obviously a desperate attempt to avoid any intimacy with him, he couldn't let it drop.

"Lauren, please." He could see the yearning for escape in her eyes but she didn't attempt to shake him off. There was something happening beneath the surface of her flippant attitude and there was something in him equally determined to find out what it was. Common sense begged him to walk away from the woman, but he ignored it. "I really would like to explain about Melanie. You still seem to believe I deliberately deceived you last night."

"What else could I think? You invite me for a moonlight walk along the beach. You kissed me —"

"And very nice it was too." What had made him blurt that out? "But may I point out that you kissed me first."

"Don't change the subject. You let me kiss you, and the next day you turn up with a baby."

"I've already explained that."

She sliced the air with her hand. "I know and I accept your explanation, okay?"

Rick shifted Melanie to his other hip and watched Lauren's eyes soften as her attention wavered toward the baby. "So, you believe I haven't got a wife hidden away somewhere?"

Her eyes moved back to his face and turned glacial again. "Yes... But I am curious about one thing. How old are you?"

He hesitated before answering, wondering where this was leading. "I'm thirty-six."

"Then why aren't you married? Are you gay?"

Rick stared at her, stunned by the question. He had been accused of a lot of things, but that wasn't one of them. He quickly recovered.

"No, I am most certainly not gay."

"Why, then?"

He blinked. "Why aren't I gay?"

"Why aren't you married?"

He smiled when he saw amusement tugging at her mouth. He didn't know where her questions were heading, and no doubt she had him in her sights, but he would play her game... for a while — if he could keep up with her changing moods.

"Not that it's any of your business, but I haven't found the right woman yet."

"And what is your 'right' woman?"

"A caring, loving lady who would be devoted to me and make a wonderful mother."

He watched the spark of mischief die from her eyes, but her face remained unchanged. He had touched a nerve, but couldn't for the life of him figure out why.

"I see. And just when do you expect to find this paragon of virtue? Time's running out. You won't be as attractive as you are now for much longer."

Something leapt in his chest at her unwitting compliment. "For your information, I did have a fiancée once."

"Really?"

"There's no need to look so surprised."

"So, what happened to her? She didn't... er... die, did she?"

"No. Actually, she ran off with my best friend."

When he saw the look of shock on her face, he was almost sorry for her. All his friends, work associates and family knew about Marion and Peter and they avoided the topic when he was around. Perhaps it was the need to talk about it with someone; someone he instinctively knew would understand that had made him confide in Lauren.

She touched his arm and he swallowed at the genuine concern in her eyes. All pretence, all artifice, had gone.

"Rick, I'm so sorry. How could any woman... why?" she finally exclaimed.

He took a deep breath. He was probably being a total fool but he decided to trust her. He shrugged, hiding the pain that still cut deep below the show of indifference. "I guess there were a number of reasons. There usually are. The one she gave me was that I was boring in bed."

"You're kidding!"

"Unfortunately, no."

"You couldn't be! I mean... I imagine... You'd be... Oh dear."

"It's okay. I'm sure she only said it in spite."

He didn't look like he really believed that. Lauren ached to reassure him that it couldn't possibly be true. That thought evoked images of him naked in her bed — images that were far from boring — and the words locked in her throat.

She reached up to touch his face, barely aware she was doing so. Melanie stared at her with huge, brown eyes. Lauren swallowed and dropped her hand again. "That's an awful thing to say," she managed lamely. "Even if it were true — and I'm not saying it is. I mean, I wouldn't know would I, you just don't seem... The way you kiss..." She stopped, feeling her cheeks go beetroot red.

He was staring at her with a strange expression on his face. Her gaze drifted over his stern features, trying to read his mind. Her mouth dried and she almost forgot to breathe.

The lunch gong sounded in the silence.

"Saved by the bell." Rick's voice was husky. His face cleared and she could see him dismiss the unpleasant memories. "I have to get some of Melanie's things for lunch," he continued. "Could you hold her for a minute while I slip back to the villa?"

Before Lauren could answer, he had deposited the baby into her arms.

"I can't." she began, but Rick had already disappeared out of earshot.

For a full minute Lauren stood fixed to the spot, willing Rick to come back. Finally, when she accepted his return wasn't imminent, she glanced around in the vain hope that someone else would rescue her. The immediate area was deserted.

She stood in the middle of the narrow sandy path. It twisted away in both directions and the palm trees lining both sides filtered the sun, providing cool dappled shade.

She looked down at Melanie. Round, innocent eyes stared back. She didn't smile at the baby and Melanie didn't smile at her. They just stared at each other. A stalemate.

She waited for the terror of a panic attack to envelop her but, apart from a slightly accelerated heartbeat, nothing happened. Even so, Lauren tried desperately to hold Melanie away from her body. Her arm soon began to ache, forcing her to maneuver the baby into a more comfortable position. She sat Melanie snugly in the crook of her arm.

The baby was heavier than she expected. She was also warm and soft. Reluctantly, Lauren looked at Melanie properly for the first time. She had a thatch of black curls, translucent, pale skin and eyes framed with long, black lashes.

Lauren was fascinated with the perfection of the tiny features. She traced the round, chubby cheeks with her fingertip, marveling at Melanie's flawless complexion. She was soon caught up in the wonder of this tiny human being. She bent and glided her own cheek over the baby's silky skin. She breathed in the warm scent of talc and something else that was uniquely baby.

Melanie reached for Lauren's hair and pulled. Lauren tried to laugh but her eyes suddenly filled with tears, the laugh turning into a strangled choke. Once started, she couldn't stop. She buried her face in the baby's neck and sobbed her heart out. Immediately, Melanie started to cry as well.

"Lauren!" Rick came running down the path, his voice filled with alarm. "What's wrong?"

Lauren was startled back to reality. Realizing what a fool she was making of herself, she quickly dumped Melanie back in Rick's arms, extricating the tiny fingers still tangled in her hair as she did so. "Nothing," she managed through her constricted throat. She turned away without meeting his eyes.

She ran to the restaurant, swiping at her wet cheeks, grateful for her dark sunglasses.

Once there, she joined the short queue at the buffet of salads, cold meat and fruit. Laden with a plate of more food than she could possibly eat, she homed in on a table of yachtsmen.

She swallowed her despair. "Hi guys," she trilled. "Got room for one more?"

"Sure, Lauren," grinned Lars, a tall Norwegian she had been talking to the night before.

She slid into a chair that would ensure her back was to the door, and Rick when he came in. She tried not to recoil at the cold chicken, ham and five different salads she had piled on her plate.

"Hungry?" teased Bob, the man on the other side of her.

She glanced at his cheeky smile. "I thought I was."

"Still feeling a bit off kilter after last night, hey?"

She bit her lip. "Um, no. What do you mean?"

There was general chuckling around the table and Lauren managed to feign a look of confusion.

"We saw you go off with that guy." Bob's wife, Maureen, was kind. "He looked nice."

Mitch, the other man, snorted and Lauren's blush deepened. "We... only went for a walk."

Lars thumped her lightly on the back. "Don't worry, your secret's safe with us. Hey, here's lover boy now."

Lauren was the only one at the table who didn't turn toward the door. She was mortified, wishing fervently she had seen sense and remained on the beach when the bell had sounded.

She heard Rick ask the waitress for a highchair for Melanie. Her heart contracted at the soft burr of his voice.

The rest of lunch was an absolute nightmare, despite the yachtsmen changing the subject to their plans to sail to other islands. Lauren forced food down her throat. She ached to run away, but didn't want to draw any more attention to herself. She should have been able to laugh off the ribald comments and teasing innuendoes, but they cut too close to the bone to be funny.

She followed the light-hearted conversation throughout lunch, laughing mechanically in all the right places. She picked at sweet cherry tomatoes and tangy tropical pasta salad, but all the time she was vitally aware of Rick and Melanie. It doesn't matter; I can do this, she chanted in her head.

She tortured herself by sneaking sidelong glances at them. She even smiled when Melanie took a handful of the stewed apple Rick was struggling to feed her and proceeded to plaster it over the highchair. But when the baby swiped her hands over her own face and in her hair causing a comical look of dismay to cross Rick's face, Lauren slid her chair back abruptly. She ran from the restaurant, ignoring the startled looks of the people at her table.

She was barely aware of her feet touching the ground as she ran down the path, forcing a young couple strolling arm in arm to leap out of her way. Once she reached her villa, she threw herself on the bed and sobbed.

"Stupid, stupid!" she cried into her pillow. She didn't know why she was so upset. Lots of people had babies. And there were plenty of men in the world she would never have. She scrubbed her eyes and tried to tell herself she was just over-tired.

"I just need some sleep and everything will look different," she reassured herself in a hiccup sob as she fell into a fitful doze.

It was with a sinking feeling in the pit of his stomach that Rick watched Lauren race from the restaurant. Her hair bounced around her shoulders, her cute butt clearly outlined through the thin fabric of her dress. He dropped the spoon that had been halfway to Melanie's mouth back into the bowl and clenched his fist in frustration. He felt the now familiar stirring in his loins. He was still perturbed by his body's instant awareness of the woman, but he ignored it with grim determination.

He concentrated instead on resisting the urge to run after her. Anything he had to say could only make matters worse. He had no idea what was wrong, but he guessed he was to blame. This morning there'd been no sign of the flirtatious party-girl of the night before. Sure, she'd tried to keep up the act but none of it had rung true. He had upset her. He was confused about exactly how he had done it, but then what did he know about women?

Melanie lost patience with the hiccup in her food supply and thumped on the highchair. Rick swung his attention back to the impatient child and laughed.

"Okay, honey, I think I get the message."

He lifted the spoon to her mouth. She allowed him to slide the apple between her lips before spitting the whole lot back out again, resuming her banging on the highchair.

He chuckled. "I guess that means you've had enough."

It still amazed him how attached to the child he had become in such a short time, how much he enjoyed looking after her. When Melanie's welfare had been thrust upon him a few days ago, his first reaction had been to reject the idea. In fact, the thought of looking after a helpless baby had scared him silly.

But, after a crash course in fatherhood by the nanny from the agency, he had not only managed fairly well with the mechanics of looking after a baby, but the child had captured his heart in the process.

He thought about the elderly folks in the homes he managed, how they'd love to meet Melanie. He wished now he'd thought to take her for a guided tour of some of the aged care facilities before he'd left Miami, but he hadn't known he'd have time. Janice and Carl were supposed to have been waiting for him on the island. Besides, he'd hardly been thinking clearly.

He undid Melanie's bib, wiped the remains of stewed apple off her hands and face and lifted her from the highchair. She clung to his pristine shirt and he shrugged fatalistically when he saw apple smears appear over the silk fabric.

"Come on, Mel. Time for a nap."

He smiled, his face softening when her eyes grew heavy and she snuggled into his neck. Why was it that babies could fall asleep at the drop of a hat, yet stayed wide awake when you were dog tired yourself?

He kissed her warm forehead and picked up the bag containing all the baby paraphernalia. He would put the child down for her afternoon nap and have a siesta himself while he worked on the merits of confronting Lauren again. Common sense told him her welfare was none of his business, but he was becoming quickly convinced the woman was a danger to her own safety. She needed looking after, no doubt about it. He didn't stop to question why he felt it was his responsibility. Or why he found himself looking for excuses to confront her.

Lauren came awake slowly. From the depths of her slumber, she could hear someone calling her name. At first she tried to ignore it, but the voice became insistent.

By the time she woke properly and realized the voice was Rick's, he was standing next to her bed.

"What are you doing here?" she asked in bewilderment. She felt hot, sticky and self-conscious. She pushed the tangle of curls out of her eyes, trying to focus on the tall figure before her.

"I came to make sure you were all right," Rick said gruffly. "It was obvious you didn't want me near you over lunch..." He paused. When she refused to fill the uneasy silence, he shrugged. "Well, I didn't want to cramp your style."

"That had nothing to do with it," she grumbled as she swung her legs off the bed.

"Anyway, you're obviously fine so I'll go now."

He didn't move. He looked around the room as if wondering how he had gotten there. He seemed uncomfortable. Well, good! She was the one who'd had her privacy invaded, so she had no intention of making it easy for him.

"Would you like me to make you coffee before I go?" he asked.

She licked her dry lips and tried to put moisture back into her parched mouth. "I'd love a beer."

He straightened. "I don't think that would be a good idea."

"Why not?" She felt like laughing at his pompous tone.

He seemed lost for words. "I... I suppose I could get you one," he mumbled eventually.

Lauren felt something move in her chest. He was kind of cute when he was unsure of himself. She felt mean for teasing him. "It's okay. I'd love a Coke actually. There should be some in the fridge. Help yourself, while you're there."

"Oh. Thanks."

When he turned his back to cross to the small fridge in the kitchenette, Lauren scanned the room for the baby, then breathed an audible sigh of relief when she was satisfied Rick had come alone. Right now, Rick was about all she could cope with. Just.

"Where's Melanie?" she couldn't resist asking as she groped for her hairbrush.

"Cathy's with her. She should sleep for two or three hours. Here," he said, handing her a cold can.

"Thanks." Lauren flipped the tab and took a grateful swig of the icy liquid before pressing the can against her hot cheeks.

Rick sat perched on the divan; Lauren climbed back on the bed and curled her legs under her.

"Er, Rick," she said after a while when the silence stretched.

"Yes?" he asked expectantly.

"I was rude earlier... about your sister, I mean. I would like to hear about her."

Rick was silent for such a long time; she started to wonder whether he'd heard her.

"I don't think so."

Lauren felt the sting of his rebuff but reminded herself it was her own fault.

"I am sorry about what I said. I didn't mean it," she persisted.

"Do you always say things you don't mean?"

Sometimes, she nearly replied before thinking better of it. She searched for another topic of conversation.

"You're from Miami, didn't you say?"

"Yes."

"What do you do? For a job, I mean."

"I'm the managing director of Corinella Aged Care."

She raised her eyebrows. "Wow, that must be challenging."

He looked at her as if wondering whether she was making fun of him before replying, "It is. I enjoy a challenge. I also enjoy knowing I can make a difference to people's lives as they grow older."

"Oh," she mumbled, feeling chastened.

She took another swig of her Coke and stared at the red, orange and yellow swirls on the bedspread. "What's your sister's name?"

He looked at her strangely before replying. "Her name was Kelsey. And she wasn't my sister, she was my aunt."

"I see." Although of course she didn't.

Rick stood up suddenly, put his drink on the table and folded his arms. "I'll leave you now. Thanks for the Coke."

Lauren jumped off the bed. She was reluctant to let him go. She had seen the flash of anguish in his eyes when he'd mentioned Kelsey and it had piqued her curiosity.

"I'd like to hear about Kelsey," she insisted as she pulled him back down to the divan so that they were sitting side by side. "Please tell me. I... I really didn't mean that silly rubbish about not wanting to have a deep and meaningful conversation with you."

"I don't know. How do I know I can trust you won't go off with your sailing buddies and have a good laugh at my expense?"

She recoiled at the harshness in his voice and she didn't much like the brutal image he had just painted of her. Did he really see her as heartless and untrustworthy? She flushed a deep red.

"All right," he said suddenly. "I'll tell you. But it's not a pretty story."

He looked at her as if waiting for an answer.

She nodded.

He hesitated a moment more before speaking. "You might have guessed that Melanie's parents aren't around anymore," he said carefully.

"I did wonder," Lauren replied.

Rick was sitting stiffly beside her with his hands clenched together between his knees. He was staring at the floor and didn't acknowledge she had spoken.

"Kelsey and Barry — he was her husband — were married for twenty years. Everyone assumed they'd never have children but then one day they announced that Kelsey was pregnant. She gave birth to Melanie two days before her fortieth birthday. They treated that baby like a princess."

He smiled but Lauren wondered if he'd forgotten she was there. He was wrapped up in the memory. She held her breath, waiting for him to go on.

"We used to tease them about making a rod for their own back, the way they spoiled her. They loved that child." He stopped again and Lauren touched him lightly on the arm. He swallowed and continued.

"Anyway, three weeks ago Kelsey and Barry were killed in a car accident. A drunk driver," Rick added bitterly.

Lauren held back a gasp.

"Thank God Melanie was home with a sitter." He sighed. "Since the accident, Barry's elderly parents have been caring for Melanie, but they're in their seventies, so it was only a temporary solution. On Kelsey's side, there's only me and my other er... sister, Janice. The obvious answer was for Janice and Carl to apply for permanent custody of Melanie. But I'm worried about Janice. She took Kelsey's death hard."

Lauren squeezed Rick's hand. "I'm sure she'll be fine in time, Rick. She just needs to come to terms with... everything."

He gave her a weak smile. "I'm sure you're right. Janice and Carl live in New York and have five children of their own, ranging from twelve to twenty-one. They were supposed to be here on the island for their first vacation alone together in years. When I arrived yesterday, there was a jumbled message from them about how they'd been delayed and instructions for me to wait here with Melanie for a few days." He sighed. "So, here I am."

"Did you travel all the way by yourself with Melanie?" Lauren asked in surprise.

He frowned. "Don't you think a thirty-six year old bachelor is capable of looking after a baby?"

"Well..."

"It's okay. Don't answer that. Actually, I had a nanny with me on the trip as far as St. Thomas. I was only meant to be on my own with Melanie for the half-hour ferry ride from there. Janice and Carl were going to be here waiting for me."

"Oh Rick, that's just awful. Poor little Melanie, all alone in the world."

She stared into Rick's eyes. They were deep and clear. She couldn't seem to drag herself away from his hard gaze.

"She's got Janice and her family," he said softly, his warm breath fanning her hot cheeks. "And she's got me," he added in a whisper.

Lauren's whole body suddenly filled with the most incredible feeling of longing. She swayed toward the man beside her and her eyelids fluttered closed.

"Lauren?" His voice seemed to come from far away.

"Yes?" she whispered.

Suddenly she was on the divan alone. Her eyes sprang open. He was standing in front of her with a strange look on his face.

"I should check Melanie. I told Cathy I wouldn't be long."

She jumped up. "That's okay," she said a little too loudly. "I've got things to do too. All this sitting around is making me bored," she said with false brightness. "I... I think I'll go out on a surf-ski. I'd ask you to come but —"

His face fell. "That's okay. You go. I don't want to bore you."

"Hey, I didn't mean..."

He shrugged. "Don't let me keep you," he said as he stood.

She hesitated, a dozen replies on the tip of her tongue. She was mortified at her rudeness, but she needed to escape. The urge to get away won over her chagrin at offending him.

With a sinking heart, she silently watched him rise and leave her villa.

When the door swung closed behind him, she quickly changed into a swimsuit and ran to the equipment shed. Her blood pumped furiously, her breath coming in short, rapid gasps.

It was only when her heartbeat slowed, and she was paddling out into the lagoon that she realized Rick hadn't explained why his sister was actually his aunt.

Three

LAUREN watched the turquoise water lap rhythmically at the side of the surf-ski. She allowed the soothing slap against the ski to lull her into a serene lassitude.

The sun beat down relentlessly; Lauren scooped up the tepid seawater and splashed it over her face and body. She was glad of the hat and sunscreen she was wearing, but the sun reflecting off the water was punishing all the same. It sapped her energy and, coupled with the gentle swell under the surf-ski, a sense of lethargy took over.

From her vantage point, she had a perfect view of the crescent shaped bay. The strip of sugar-white sand was fringed with tall coconut palms and she could just make out the villas, with their thatched roofs, dotted amongst the trees.

She turned her head slowly toward the distant shore. Rick was standing at the water's edge with another man. She waved to him. He lifted his arm in response, and then made hand signals indicating he wanted her to return to the beach.

She laughed and waved back again, ignoring his silly request.

"I'm not ready for the real world," she said to herself. Rick's story had upset and unnerved her more than she wanted to admit. She didn't have any siblings of her own and the thought of Rick losing his sister like that was too awful to contemplate. The knowledge that Melanie would never know her mother stabbed at Lauren's soft heart.

She tried to put the sad story to the back of her mind

and her thoughts turned to Rick. But that was dangerous ground indeed. She didn't want to think about how he made her feel. It's only physical attraction, she reassured herself. Then why did her heart leap each time he came near?

She was glad she'd come out here on the water. She needed this peace and serenity to assimilate the emotions tangled around her heart. With only the tropical fish and sea birds for company, she was in no hurry to return to the human race.

Eventually she realized that she could barely make out the figures still standing on the shore; she had floated out past the entrance to the lagoon. Lauren tightened her grip on the paddle and started to idly guide the surf-ski closer to shore.

When she made no headway, she increased the pace and acknowledged it would probably be a good idea to return to the protection of the bay. At the same time, she realized the water was no longer lapping quietly at the watercraft, but had become an insistent nudge that jolted her from side to side.

The surf-ski was being propelled further toward the open ocean without any help from her.

Rick had been watching her for a long time. At first she had paddled idly around the small bay but for the last fifteen minutes she hadn't made any attempt to steer. In fact, she seemed to be just staring into the water.

His face was stiff as he turned to Jeff, the resort skipper standing next to him. "Is she all right?" he asked tightly.

Jeff, a short, wiry man of indeterminate age, in long khaki shorts and black singlet, folded his arms and frowned. "Not sure," he drawled slowly. "If she strays too far into Cruz Bay she might not be. The water rushes along that channel between St. Thomas and St. John, at eight knots some days. If the tide is ebbing she could end up anywhere.

Rick's gut clenched. He couldn't understand how the man next to him could appear so calm. "Do you think –"?

Jeff rubbed his chin. "Yes, I'd say it's about time I made sure she isn't in trouble. Sometimes guests go around the headland to the next bay, but I'm not confident your friend has the strength or experience to do it safely."

He turned away and headed up the beach to where a small dinghy with an outboard motor attached was hauled up on the sand. As he started to drag it toward the water, Rick quickly stepped in to help, pushing the boat into water deep enough for Jeff to fire up the motor.

By the time the dinghy was well afloat and the motor chugging, Lauren had disappeared from view.

Rick stood on the shore staring at the empty horizon for two full seconds before his body galvanized into action. He ploughed through the water, uncaring of the damage the salt water would do to his expensive leather sandals.

"I'm coming with you!" he called to Jeff and hauled himself into the boat, causing it to rock violently.

"Okay. Sit tight."

Rick clung grimly to the side of the boat, all the while scanning the edge of the bay and the channel.

To his relief, it was only minutes before they reached the headland. They spotted Lauren immediately. She was rowing furiously but the current was pulling her further into the fast moving waters of the passage.

"She's caught on the turning tide," Jeff called to Rick. "But, don't worry, we'll have her in a minute."

Despite the confidence in Jeff's voice, a tense knot of fear twisted in Rick's stomach.

He kept his eyes glued on Lauren while Jeff skillfully maneuvered the boat. In no time they were beside Lauren and her small surf-ski. She had been so intent on her task, she didn't notice their presence until Jeff called out. When she turned, the relief on her face was obvious.

She grinned and said cheerfully, "Hi, fancy meeting you here."

Rick leaned between the boat and Lauren, helping her clamber across to the dinghy, while Jeff secured the surf-ski.

"You stupid woman!" Rick exploded.

Lauren's face fell. Her eyes shimmered with tears and Rick felt sick to his stomach.

Before he could open his mouth to apologize, she fell into his arms sobbing, "I'm sorry. I'm sorry."

Rick was floored by this total turnaround in behavior. A sliver of doubt edged its way into his brain. The woman was a mass of contradictions, but right now she was obviously upset, despite her flippant attitude to her rescue. He cursed his insensitivity and gathered her close to his chest.

"What am I going to do with you?" he murmured into her hair.

Jeff steered the dinghy into the shore, jumping out of the boat when it reached the shallows of the lagoon. Rick gently put Lauren away from him and slipped into the water to help Jeff. Once the bottom of the boat scraped the seabed, he leaned in, scooped Lauren into his arms and waded with her the last few yards to the sand.

"Thanks, skipper," he said to Jeff as he eased Lauren carefully to her feet. "We owe you one."

"Is she okay?" Jeff said over his shoulder as he secured the boat.

"Just a bit shaken. She'll be alright once she's rested."

"No problem. Just watch for the symptoms of sunstroke, though. Even a mild dose can cause high temperature, nausea, clammy skin, that sort of thing."

Lauren watched the exchange in silence. She was feeling much better now that she was back safely on land. She knew she hadn't been in any real danger, but it had shaken her up all the same.

"You can come and rescue me anytime." She smiled sheepishly at Jeff to cover up her embarrassment. She knew her eyes were red and swollen and her hair was a mass of salty tangles.

Jeff grinned and winked at her. "Glad to be of service."

"Thanks again," called Rick gruffly as Jeff walked back up the beach.

Rick grabbed Lauren's arm and spun her around. "What is it with you?" he ground out. "Do you aim to seduce every male under eighty on the island?"

Lauren stared at him in bewilderment. "If you disapprove of me so much, why do you stay around me?"

"I don't disapprove exactly –" He stopped.

She watched his face carefully, trying to read his mind but it was impossible.

"Yes?" she asked sarcastically. "Go on."

"I'm sorry if I gave you that impression," he said finally. "It's not you I disapprove of, it's just the way you... throw yourself at people."

She tried flippancy to cover up her hurt. "Jealous?"

"Hardly."

"Well, thanks very much."

Rick seemed to suddenly realize how he had sounded. "Look, Lauren, you're a lovely young woman and your... style would suit most men. But..."

"Not you."

"I was going to say, but some might get the wrong idea."

"What if I wanted them to get the idea?"

Rick frowned. "Well, that would be none of my business."

"I could make it your business." She touched his bare arm with her fingertips, gliding them over his hot skin.

"This is not a game – you could have drowned." He stopped and the word hung between them.

"If I didn't know better, I'd think you cared," said Lauren finally. *Why do I persist in making sure he thinks the worst of me*? She already regretted her silly words. She had no idea what had made her say them. Except that she wanted to cover up what she knew had been an irresponsible thing to do in allowing the surf-ski to drift so far. Stupidly, she'd hoped to convince both men she'd had the situation under control all along.

"Don't get any ideas," Rick snarled.

Lauren suddenly felt exhausted and her head throbbed. "I don't... feel so good," she whispered. "I... I think I need to lie down."

"Yes, perhaps you should," Rick said gruffly. "And I hope you'll think twice before doing anything so stupid again."

She was dredging her brain for something rude to snap back in reply when she looked into his eyes. Despite his rough words she couldn't mistake the concern she saw there. Her heart went soft and for long seconds everything around them faded away. She forgot about feeling sick and in need of a shower and a lie down. She was trapped by the mesmerizing gaze in his eyes.

"I... I'm sorry," she said in a voice that hardly seemed to belong to her. "You're right. I was stupid."

"I didn't say you were stupid, only –" Rick began before he realized her eyes had fluttered closed.

"What are you doing?" Lauren woke suddenly and jarringly to find needles of cold water biting into her flesh.

"Sorry, but I needed to get your body temperature down. Jeff could be right about the sunstroke. Now, strip off that swimsuit and I'll rinse it out for you."

Lauren was truly startled by the idea before she realized he wasn't making a pass. Then she felt silly. "Forget it, pal," she managed.

He looked affronted. "I won't look."

"That's what they all say."

"They do?"

The expression on his face was quite comical but she was in no mood to tease him further. She shook her head in exasperation then realized she had a thumping headache and winced. "How would I know?" she finally grumbled.

"Head hurt?"

"Yes. And I feel sick."

"Jeff said to make sure you have plenty of fluids and salt. Now strip off, like a good girl, and I'll find something for your headache." He turned away, closing the bathroom door behind him.

Lauren bit back a retort. "Forget what Jeff said," she growled under her breath.

Knowing she was wasting the island's precious water while she stood there fuming, she took advantage of Rick's absence and quickly did as he'd instructed. She tossed the sodden Lycra out of the cubicle onto the tiled floor, and then reached for the shampoo.

She stared in confusion at the unfamiliar label on the bottle. When she realized why it wasn't the brand she used, embarrassment flooded her body. She obviously wasn't in her own villa. She must be in his.

Anticipating Rick's possible return, she finished washing her hair in record time and turned off the water. She peered out of the cubicle hoping he was in the habit of using extra-large bath towels.

To her relief, a navy toweling robe was hanging from the hook behind the bathroom door. She quickly slipped into it, lifting her long hair out, hiding her slim figure in its voluminous folds. She cursed her body's instant reaction to the male scent lingering in the plush cloth.

With any luck, he would allow her to go next-door to retrieve her own clothes with a minimum of fuss and maximum of dignity. But, to her surprise and relief, when she came out of the bathroom, the main room, furnished identically to her own, was empty.

She expelled a lungful of air and started for the door. It was then that she noticed the crib and the baby, sound asleep inside. She was lying on her back in nothing but a singlet and diaper. Damp curls clung to her forehead and her tiny mouth was open.

Lauren's body flooded with tension, she spun on her heels, scanning the room again in the vain hope that Rick was there after all.

Her eyes alighted on a piece of paper that had writing scrawled across it. She snatched it up, her heart sinking before she had even scanned the contents.

Lauren. Gone to get painkillers. Please watch Melanie. Cathy had to go. Help yourself to the fridge. Back soon. Rick.

"Isn't that just terrific," she ground out. He'd made sure she couldn't run next door to her villa even for the few minutes it would take to retrieve her clothes.

She sat on the edge of the bed and waited. She willed

the baby not to wake up as tension snaked through her body. She looked around the room. The navy trousers that Rick had been wearing the night before were hung neatly over the back of a chair, but that was where the tidiness ended. The rest of the room was a muddle of baby clothes, open packets of disposable diapers and baby toys. She had the distinct impression that Rick's world was normally without its current state of lovable chaos.

Suddenly remembering her thirst, she headed for the minibar, grateful for something to do. She poured herself a glass of orange juice and drank.

Feeling much better, she decided it was ridiculous to sit primly on the edge of the bed when her body was pleading for rest. She knew from experience that panic attacks were most likely when she was over-tired and her brain too exhausted to cope. Besides, if Jeff was right about her suffering from a touch of sun, the best thing she could do was lie down.

She fell back onto the pillows, sighing into the softness of the mattress. "Just for a minute," she murmured before she succumbed to a deep sleep.

As Rick took the steps to his villa two at a time, he mentally adjusted his demeanor from happy anticipation to indifferent detachment. His heart leapt at the thought that he would find Lauren ensconced in his villa but he squashed the feeling as fanciful nonsense. There was no reason for the elation bubbling along his bloodstream.

He was greeted with silence as he quietly opened and closed the screen-door and carefully placed the small packet of headache tablets and the bottle of sports drink on the table.

He cast his eyes around the room, alighting first on Melanie, stirring in the crib, and then Lauren, spread-eagled across the bed on her stomach. He cursed his body's instinctive response as he took in her smooth, tanned legs and hair tumbling in riotous abandon over the pillow.

He gulped as he realized that his bathrobe, which should have ensured complete modesty, had ridden up her thighs and was only inches away from displaying a delectable, naked rump.

He swore silently and turned away. An image of his mother's face, lips pursed, planted itself in his brain. She would have expected his behavior in such an untenable situation to be above reproach. His mother...

It was over twenty years since Eleanor had died and just as long since he'd discovered, too late, that she was really his grandmother.

But sometimes, the pain that had swamped his body the day he had discovered the lies was as fresh as if it were yesterday. Since his grandmother's death, he'd often wondered why she had kept the diaries, and concluded that she wanted him to know... to discover the truth. She had obviously had her own reasons for not telling him herself.

He often wished she had taken her secret to the grave. Far better to think his mother was cold and unfeeling. Better than the truth. That she was a drug addict who had died when he was five years old. He had only the dimmest memory of his real mother, the woman he had believed to be his glamorous sister.

Melanie started to stir again. Rick swallowed. His mouth felt like fine dry sandpaper. "Pull yourself together," he muttered before crossing the room to the minibar.

The nanny had given him precise instructions on Melanie's routine. He knew the baby wasn't due for a feed but, because of the humid climate he opted to give her some watered down juice.

Setting a saucepan of water to boil with the baby bottle standing up in it, he picked up Melanie before she started to bellow and wake Lauren.

He kissed the child on the forehead, enjoying the closeness of the small body. He had been horrified when he'd first realized he would have the baby to care for. Now, he didn't relish giving her up to Janice and Carl. In such a short time he had become so attached to Melanie, his mind turned away from the thought of the separation that would come with the arrival of his sister and her husband.

But Melanie deserved a real family. She deserved everything Kelsey and Barry would have wanted for her, and more.

Once the bottle was sterilized and juice topped up with bottled water added, Rick propped himself up against the bed-head, only inches from Lauren's unconscious body. It was madness, but he ignored common sense.

At first he tried to pretend that Lauren's semi-naked body wasn't beside him. He concentrated on Melanie's eager gulps. By the time the baby started to nod off again, he had given up willpower as a bad joke and allowed himself the dubious luxury of feasting his eyes on the woman that was destined to send him insane.

She was gorgeous, but in sleep the feisty irreverence softened to vulnerability that made Rick's heart clench. The woman drove him crazy one minute and made him laugh at his own stuffiness the next.

Desperate to control his wayward thoughts, he gently eased Melanie onto the cool sheet between himself and Lauren. Then he snatched up his book from the bedside table.

"Organizational Change in a Contemporary Society. Should be more effective than a cold shower," he said wryly to himself before opening the thick volume at the spot he had left his bookmark.

He stared at the words, reading the same paragraph several times before he gave up the pretence. He sighed deeply and closed his eyes. "Either God is having a joke at my expense or this is a very bad dream that I'll wake up from at any time," he mumbled. "Either way, if this woman doesn't drive me insane, it'll be a miracle."

Rick heard Melanie crying from the depths of a half sleeping state. He didn't open his eyes. She was hungry of course and he had to get up to feed her, but his body begged for just a few more seconds' sleep.

He recalled how, only a week before the accident, Kelsey had been boasting that Melanie had, at last, been sleeping through the night. Ever since the accident, though, she had taken to waking every four hours and nothing short of a bottle would settle her down again.

Suddenly he felt the bed move, heard a startled gasp, then a loud accusatory demand.

"How could you? How could you?"

Melanie's cries became insistent bellows. Simultaneously he remembered several things. It was not the middle of the night. It was probably early evening. And Lauren was in bed with him.

Before he had a chance to fully absorb the implications of these pieces of information, he was being shaken violently.

He sat up, pushing the hair from his forehead and flexing his cramped shoulder muscles. "Lauren! What on earth is wrong?"

"I told you I couldn't be around babies!"

He suddenly became fully awake as he looked into her stricken face. His heart shifted uncomfortably in his chest as he blurted the first unguarded words that sprang to mind. "Lauren, I'm sorry, honey, but I just don't believe you. Please tell me what's wrong. Maybe I can help."

Lauren watched Rick pick up Melanie and struggle to ease himself off the bed with the screaming baby. Her own nerves screamed in unison, butterflies going berserk in her stomach.

She leapt off the bed. "No-one can help. Not unless you can erase the last six months of my life!" She felt the familiar surge of panic race through her body as the need to escape overrode every other thought process. Nausea sat like thick glue in her stomach and the air lodged in her throat making it difficult to breathe.

"Lauren, please don't go –" Rick called as she charged out of his villa to the safety of hers.

As soon as she reached her villa, Lauren snatched up the medication her therapist had prescribed in the unlikely event she would need them while she was on vacation. She had jokingly referred to them as her "panic pills" but they were her safety net, her security blanket and, right now, her lifeline.

She got as far as pushing the small tablet from its foil packet before she stopped herself. What was she? A woman or a mouse? How could she let something as harmless as a baby turn her into a nutcase?

She took three deep, calming breaths then reached for the switch to the kettle. It wasn't the baby. Well, not entirely. Rick was to blame. He had walked into the restaurant – was it really less than twenty-four hours ago? – and turned her newly sorted life into an uncontrolled mess. He was turning her into a basket case.

Lauren tossed the tablet, still clutched in her clammy

hand, into the sink and dropped heavily into a chair. In all honesty, she couldn't blame Rick for her sudden and inexplicable over-reaction to perfectly normal situations.

She had woken on his bed practically naked with a baby next to her. So what. That didn't mean she had to react as if she expected the baby to turn into a character from a horror movie, for heaven's sake!

The kettle boiled and she poured the steaming water over an herbal tea bag, a drink she had taken to for its calming effects. While she waited for the tea to brew, she shrugged off Rick's bathrobe, dressed in navy shorts and crossover halter-top, dragging a brush through her tangled hair.

As she inhaled the fragrant steam and sipped at the hot liquid, she practiced the deep breathing exercises her therapist had taught her. By the time the cup was empty, she was feeling almost back to normal. So normal, in fact, she felt entirely silly about the whole episode.

Her gut reaction was to act as if nothing untoward had transpired next time she saw Rick. The more realistic side of her knew she would have to at least apologize for her odd behavior.

She finished brushing the knots from her hair and caught it up in a band high on her head. Taking another deep breath, she picked up Rick's bathrobe, left the villa and covered the short distance to his villa.

She could hear the deep burr of Rick's voice through the open louvers as he spoke quietly to Melanie. Evidently, her bottle was finished and he was offering her a baby cookie. She hesitated at the door.

Lauren took a deep breath before calling out in a tentative voice, "Hi! Anyone home?" She could see Rick settling the baby into a high chair through the wire screen and cursed herself for the inane question.

Her heart hammered wildly in her chest, she was becoming so used to her body's eager anticipation whenever she was near Rick, she barely noticed.

Rick turned. "So, the prodigal returns," he said dryly as he crossed the room to open the door for her.

"I... I came to apologize. I think I overreacted."

"You'd better come in," he said quietly, taking the offered bathrobe from her.

She hesitated on the threshold. "I... I'm sorry about before."

He nodded. He looked rather unsure himself and Lauren almost turned and ran away again.

"You'd better come in," he said again, eventually holding the door open for her.

She still didn't move. She looked past him to where Melanie was sitting with soggy cookie covering half her face, chewing the remains, and her fist, at the same time. Lauren swallowed, trying to put moisture into her dry mouth.

"I... I don't think –"

Rick gently took her arm and tugged her inside. "She won't bite, you know," he said solemnly.

Lauren's head snapped up and she glared at him. "I know that!"

"What's the problem then?"

"Who said there was a problem?"

"You did. You said you hated babies. I wouldn't call that exactly normal. Would you?"

"Plenty of people don't like babies."

"But not you."

She thought of denying the simple statement. He didn't know anything. He was only guessing. But suddenly it all seemed so pointless. Maybe if she explained, he would understand her dilemma and keep away from her.

Then she wouldn't have to worry about the awful possibility of falling in love...

She squashed the thought. "No, not me," she whispered while she stared at her feet.

Rick touched her chin and lifted her head gently. "Do you want to talk about it?"

"You'll think I'm insane, or at least stupid."

A pained expression crossed his face. "There's a lot of conclusions I could draw about you, but that isn't one of them."

She tested a half smile but she didn't think she pulled it off. Her heart leapt like a fish. *I hope I'm not making a huge mistake*.

Rick drew her inside the villa and closed the screen-door behind her.

"Rick! Are you in there?"

Lauren turned, startled at the female voice coming from the porch. Rick groaned. "Cathy," he said by way of explanation.

Lauren's face relaxed.

"Come in," called Rick.

Cathy burst in the door, panting. She had obviously just run down the path. "The dinner bell will ring in a few minutes. I came to see whether you need me this evening or –" She stopped when she suddenly registered Lauren's presence.

"Hi! Lauren, isn't it?"

Lauren smiled at the young girl's cheerfulness. "Yes. Nice to see you again."

Cathy nodded and turned back to Rick. "I guess you'll be wanting a babysitter tonight," she grinned.

Rick looked taken aback at Cathy's innocent assumption. He said nothing for several seconds. Lauren held her breath as a number of unidentifiable expressions crossed his face.

He suddenly seemed to make up his mind. "No, I won't need you tonight, thank you. But could you do me a favor?"

"Sure."

"Could you arrange for dinner to be brought to the villa? For two," he added stiffly.

Lauren's eyes widened. He was embarrassed! A quiver of excitement tingled along her veins. She half-heartedly pushed it away but the happy anticipation in her heart wouldn't be silenced. He wanted to be alone with her! Okay, so Melanie would be chaperon, but...

"Would you like a bottle of champagne, too?" asked Cathy with a cheeky grin.

"No!" Rick choked out, much to Lauren's amusement. "Er, that won't be necessary," he added more calmly. "Liquor doesn't agree with Lauren."

Lauren swallowed a giggle but she couldn't prevent the corners of her mouth from twitching. Cathy raised her eyebrows and looked from one to the other. Lauren waited for Cathy to dispute the statement – after all, she had seen Lauren indulging quite freely all week without mishap – but she apparently thought better of it when she saw Rick's grim face.

"No problem," she said with a smirk. "I'll bring your meals shortly."

"Thanks," Rick said sternly as he shepherded her to the door.

After Cathy had skipped away down the steps and Rick had closed the door again with a snap, Lauren suddenly broke into a fit of giggles.

"What's so funny?" he growled.

She tried to sober up but his pompous expression sent her into giggles again. "You!"

"Oh?" he asked ominously.

"You're worried it'll be all over the island that we're carrying on a torrid affair."

"I am not," he said indignantly. "The possibility never crossed my mind."

"Darn it," she murmured.

He raised his eyebrows and Lauren cursed her big mouth.

"Perhaps this wasn't such a good idea," Rick ground out in a tone he normally reserved for pulling recalcitrant employees into line.

Actually, he was positive inviting Lauren to stay with him for dinner was an extremely bad idea. He hadn't been able to handle her fresh effervescence last night, so what made him think anything had changed?

He was well aware of his own shortcomings, especially from the female point of view. He imagined most people saw him as, at best, stodgy and, at worst, implacable. He was a fool to try and be something he wasn't. Yes, he was a fool, but that didn't stop him being drawn to Lauren.

He watched Lauren's face fall and her cheeks flush, but he refused to take back the arrogant words. Even so, her flippant retort seemed to mask hidden depths he had yet to plumb. He didn't know why he felt a compulsion to decipher the mixed messages.

Lauren was almost at the door before Rick said quietly, "Running away again?"

She spun around with a scowl on her face. "I know when I'm not wanted."

He frowned. She was giving him the perfect escape route. It would be so easy to let her flounce out of his life, but that dreaded magnetic pull was doing its work on him again. Hell, how he hated being unsure of himself. He was floundering. He knew it. He hated it. But he couldn't help it. There was something about her that was irresistible.

"Are you giving up that easily? Up until now, you struck me as a fighter," he said calmly.

He read the confusion in her eyes and for a minute thought he'd revealed too much. Did she sense he was toying with the idea of a possible relationship?

All of a sudden, she seemed to gather something within herself. "Yes, I am a fighter. And I've put up with too much trash in my life to put up with any more from you. You see things in black and white. Right and wrong. I'm sure when you're at work you say 'jump', and your underlings say 'how high'!"

"Not all of them. But, then, those particular employees don't work for me any more."

At her look of horror, he almost laughed. "I was joking," he added quickly.

She tossed her hair over her shoulder in the same way he remembered from the night before. He sucked in his breath at the memory the action stirred. Don't even try to resist, pal. You're already doomed.

"Okay, I'll stay," Lauren said finally. "But if I feel like leaving at any time, I will."

Rick let out the breath he had been holding. "Fine." He didn't know if he felt relieved or cursed.

Nothing more was said between them while Rick sorted out Melanie. Lauren cleared the small table ready for dinner.

Rick wiped the gooey cookie from Melanie's chubby fingers then carefully cleaned her face. Lauren didn't offer to help, but after the few cryptic remarks she had made about babies, he wasn't surprised.

However, he could feel her eyes on him, he knew she watched his every move as he changed Melanie's diaper and dressed her for bed.

She didn't even speak when he laughed at the way

Melanie's legs kicked in all directions while he tried to maneuver them into the pink stretch suit.

He longed to coax Lauren to join in the tickling game he played with the baby before he finally settled her into bed. But his head told him to steer clear of the woman and her problems. He had no idea how to handle her. In short, he had no wish to involve himself in her life.

So why had he invited her to dinner?

And why, even as he tucked the soft blanket around Melanie and kissed the baby's tender cheek, were his thoughts filled with the memory of kissing Lauren?

Four

♡

DESPITE Lauren's misgivings, dinner was a pleasant affair. It consisted of a variety of dishes, including guacamole, fajitas, re-fried beans and corn-on-the-cob. The resort's restaurant regularly had a theme night and this evening, it was Mexican.

Despite Rick's earlier acerbic comments about Lauren and liquor, he produced a bottle of full-bodied red wine to go with the meal. It went a long way to contributing to the genial atmosphere.

After the first sip, Lauren was grateful for the mellowing effect the smooth merlot had on her nerves. However, once her guard relaxed, her body took it as a signal to pull out all the stops.

Her senses sprang to full alert. Her eyes followed every move Rick made. As he cut his food, she was fixated with his large, rugged hands. She couldn't shift her gaze from his squarely cut fingernails, the hard sinews and dark hairs on the back of his hands.

She remembered how those strong fingers had stroked her super-sensitive skin, alighting nerve endings and leaving a trail of fire that had yet to be quenched.

Wrenching her eyes away from his hands, Lauren's gaze swept up to his mouth. His oh-so-kissable mouth. As he swallowed a mouthful of food, his eyes lifted to hers. She didn't look away. She couldn't. A burning, all-consuming need for his hands, for his mouth, robbed her of all coherent thought.

"Not eating?" Rick queried mildly.

Lauren felt her already heated cheeks burn and

quickly forked some food into her mouth. It prevented her from having to answer his question. She very much doubted any rational words would have made their way past the lump in her throat anyway.

A wild, reckless imp teased her imagination. She saw herself toss caution out the window and let it blow away on the ocean breeze. She would be free then, free to allow all the pent-up longings to burst from her body. She licked her lips and tried to moisten her parched mouth.

Visions of Rick shedding his proper persona and scooping her into his arms splashed across her mind in stark detail. He would bury his face in her neck and nibble on her racing pulse. She would gasp with desire. He would groan with an overpowering need for her. *Make love to me*! she would beg.

"Lauren?"

For one, crazy split second Lauren thought she'd spoken the words aloud. She whipped her head up, alarmed to find herself staring into deep pools of melting-chocolate brown. She felt like a rabbit caught in the headlights of an SUV bearing down at speed. She was unable to break free from the mesmerizing spell.

Lauren felt her longing reciprocated as she sensed Rick's desire like a live wire arcing between them. He wanted her. She could feel it. It made her nervous but, at the same time, she reveled in the raw, female power.

The tension made her giddy. She snatched at her wine glass and took a healthy gulp. When she next looked at him, his full attention was back on his food. It made her feel strangely deflated. She shook off the feeling, but an uncomfortable sensation of something unfinished remained.

As Rick cleared their empty plates, he suddenly asked the one question Lauren had hoped he had forgotten.

"Now that I've fed you, do you want to tell me about your aversion to children?"

"I have no aversion to children," she snapped before she realized, too late, what she had revealed by her impetuous words.

"Now we get to the truth of it."

"Not in the way you're referring to, anyway," she added more carefully.

Rick ran water into the sink over the dishes then came back to the table. "If you've changed your mind about discussing your problems, fine. I have no intention of prying."

Lauren slid her finger down the side of her glass of iced water, leaving a trail in the droplets of condensation. "You wouldn't understand."

"You might be surprised. But if you don't want to... Perhaps we should call it a night."

Rick held his breath, hoping she wouldn't leave. He was terrified he would say the wrong thing. Everything would be a lot easier if she left. His pulse rate would go back to normal, for one.

And how did she see him? he wondered. Safe? Boring?

He waited. The need to understand her had strengthened. He told himself it was just curiosity, but...

"It's hard to know where to begin," Lauren said eventually. She took a small sip of water.

Rick's heart softened at the look of pain on her face. The naked desire for her ebbed slightly and was replaced by a tender ache.

He looked at her blandly, hoping she couldn't read his thoughts. "The beginning usually works best," he said with what he hoped was the right amount of encouragement.

"Ah, but where does it all begin – really?"

He said nothing.

Lauren sighed and rubbed her temple. She took a deep breath. "My mother died from cancer when I was twelve."

He was startled by the blunt statement. His heart went out to her, but he didn't reveal his thoughts.

"I'm sorry," he said.

Melanie moved restlessly and Lauren glanced over to the crib. When the baby settled again, she returned her attention to Rick, but she didn't meet his eyes.

"I think I know a little of how you feel," Rick prompted. "The woman I knew as my mother died when I was sixteen."

She lifted her eyes to him before quickly averting her gaze again. He imagined she was waiting for him to elaborate, but he didn't. He had a sudden impulse to tell her about his own family. But, right now, he yearned to know more about this contradictory woman. His own turbulent background could wait.

"As a teenager, I hated my father," she said when he didn't elaborate. "I thought it was his fault my mother had died. I believed he should have been able to do something to stop it happening. She was in terrible pain close to the end. I hated him for that too... and a lot of other things. Some of those feelings weren't very rational, I guess."

"And now? How do you feel about him?"

She seemed lost in thought for a minute before the wistful expression on her face disappeared. "I don't even know why I'm telling you this. You sound like my therapist!"

He was startled by her sudden outburst, but he also felt like laughing out loud. She had such a passionate spirit. Despite anything else he thought about her, he had to admire her fire. He couldn't imagine this woman ever wallowing in self-pity. He couldn't think of what to say. He was out of his depth again. It proved she was totally wrong for him. Thank goodness he was able to stay detached and keep his emotions under control.

"I'm sorry," he said lamely.

"No, you're not."

He tried another tack. "You don't have to talk about it, you know. I just thought it would help. Talking can put your problems into perspective. I don't pretend to understand, but in my line of work I come across people with varied backgrounds. Some of them have emotional problems through being rejected by their families."

Lauren stood up suddenly and paced the room then sat down again with a plop. "Do you know how pompous you sound? You really think you've got me all worked out, don't you?"

"I would never be so presumptuous."

"Now you *are* taking a shot at me."

"Not at all."

"I think I'll have coffee." She jumped out of her seat again.

Rick stood up. "Sit down. I'll get it. It is my room after all, what sort of host allows a guest to get her own coffee?"

Lauren sat again. "Sorry," she said grumpily.

Rick moved over to the kitchenette and spooned coffee granules into mugs. "Do you want to tell me about your father," he asked over his shoulder.

"Let's just say he made my life hell. So much so, even Brian Butterfield looked like a knight in shining armor," she said with a touch of resentment in her voice.

"Brian?"

"My ex-fiancé."

"That Brian."

"Bastard," she muttered under her breath.

He turned to look at her. "I am?"

She grimaced. "Not you. Brian. I thought he was a dream come true. Too bad he turned out to be little better than my father."

The kettle boiled and Rick poured steaming water into the mugs. "Cream? Sugar?"

Lauren nodded distractedly. "Yes, thanks."

Rick carefully dropped a measure of cream into each mug, carried them to the table and sat down. He then leaned back and reached over to the bench for the jar of sugar sachets and placed them on the table between them.

Lauren absently plucked one of the sachets out, tore off the top and sprinkled the sugar over the steaming coffee.

She took a few sips from her mug before she said, "My therapist convinced me I could do whatever I wanted with my life."

"Smart therapist."

She raised her eyebrows. "I used to think being married to Brian was what I wanted. I see now I only became engaged to escape from my father. My therapist made me realize I had the strength to survive without Brian or my father. Although, I have to admit that since my father disowned me, it's been easier to break away from his oppressive authority." She laughed as if she didn't care.

When Rick's face remained somber, her grin fell.

"It hurts, doesn't it?" he asked quietly.

"Sometimes," Lauren admitted. "I think the hardest thing was that when it came to the crunch, Brian took my father's side.

"My father had always said I would come to a bad end.

I constantly disobeyed him, you see. Especially after Mom died. But he was so unfair! Sometimes I would go into the city and stay in the mall for hours just to get away from his black moods, even knowing I would be locked in my room without dinner when I got home."

"Did he... beat you?"

Lauren stirred her coffee for the second time. "No. He never went that far. He just ranted on and on. Brian had always sympathized with me; referred to my father as a tyrant. I expected him to stand by me always. I... I thought he cared for me."

She swallowed a mouthful of coffee but didn't look up.

"You loved him," Rick said simply.

She shook her head. "I thought I did. Maybe he was just a way of escaping from my father. At the time, I thought it was love. And I thought he loved me. We met at a church youth group. He used to say it was my enthusiasm for life that attracted him to me in the first place. It was my *exuberance*," – Lauren sneered the word – "that he admired. He said I had rescued him from falling into a pit of 'absurd intellectuality'." She laughed scornfully, "His words, not mine."

"Do I remind you of him?"

She lifted her head and stared at Rick as if seeing him for the first time. "Of course not!" she protested eventually. "You're... you're nothing like him."

Rick lifted one eyebrow. "Methinks the lady doth protest too much," he said with heavy irony. "Earlier you were calling me pompous. Correct me if I'm wrong, but that particular adjective seems to fit Brian's character."

Lauren sighed and sipped her coffee.

Rick held his breath. For some reason totally beyond his comprehension, her opinion of him suddenly took on vital importance.

"Rick..." she began.

"Yes?" he whispered.

"I... I'm sorry for saying that. You're nothing like Brian. Not... where it matters. Inside. You would never do what he did."

A dozen possibilities of the meaning behind Lauren's words tumbled over each other in Rick's mind. What would he never do? He nearly asked her, but what if it was something he *would* do? He cringed at the thought.

How he longed to know how Lauren really saw him. He cursed Marion, his ex-fiancée, for the hundredth time. The woman was bitter and twisted and he knew she had insulted him out of pure spite but no matter how much he rationalized it, the seed of doubt refused to die.

Lauren was so beautiful, vibrant and sexy. One minute he thought she was coming on to him and the next... he wasn't so sure. Either way, despite the desire that increased every time he saw her, he couldn't make love to her.

She deserved a man with the same vitality as herself, not someone like him; starched and pressed into the mold fashioned by his grandmother. She deserved a man with no baggage who would nurture her, love her, and treat her like a precious jewel.

"Rick..." she whispered. "I want to tell you what happened. I need to tell you."

Rick picked up her hand and squeezed it. "You can."

Her eyes suddenly filled with tears. "Brian and I were going to get married. Or should I say *I* wanted to get married. Brian kept putting it off..."

"And?" he encouraged.

"He was the first man I ever... slept with." She blinked and the tears spilled onto her cheeks. "He... he wanted to wait, but... I... I..."

"It's okay. It's nothing to be ashamed of." Who was he to say that? He had slotted her into the mold of a shameless hussy. How could he have been so arrogant?

"We only did it once. I... didn't like it much."

Rick blushed to the roots of his hair. He didn't want to hear this. He didn't want to think about her being touched at all!

"He... He said it wasn't right. I had tempted him and he was ashamed." She was openly sobbing now but Rick was glued to his chair. He couldn't move.

"When I found out I was pregnant, he didn't want to know me."

"Pregnant?" Rick nearly choked on the word. "But... the... baby?"

"It's gone."

"Gone?" he said in confusion.

She looked up at him. Tears were streaming down her face and her eyes were awash. "I had a miscarriage. My... my baby died."

With awful clarity, Rick saw everything Lauren had said and done since they had met in a different light. He suddenly came alive and shook off the mire of confusion surrounding his brain. He pulled Lauren gently up from the chair and swept her against his body. "Oh, honey. I didn't know. I'm so sorry."

No wonder she had looked hunted every time she was near Melanie!

Lauren didn't seem to hear him. She sobbed against his chest, soaking his shirt.

"You're young. There'll be other babies. With a man who deserves your love." *Idiot! What sort of inane statement is that?*

"No –"

Rick gathered her more tightly into his arms and

swallowed her words with his own mouth as he kissed her with exquisite tenderness. A wave of protectiveness washed over him.

"I'm sorry," he murmured against her mouth. "That was an incredibly stupid and insensitive thing to say."

She shook her head. Tears were still streaming down her face, but she didn't seem to notice. "No. It's not that. You don't understand."

"Hush. It's okay. You don't have to tell me any more."

He held her against his body, smoothing her hair and whispering soothing words in her ear. To think she had lost her baby *and* her fiancé. Not to mention the censure she had obviously received from her own father. And here was he, Mr. High-and-mighty, making rash judgments about her behavior.

The woman was obviously still grieving. Her flirting was probably just a cover-up for all the hurt and disillusionment. And he had tramped all over her emotions with his size ten boots.

Rick kept her enfolded in his arms for several minutes until he was alerted to the increasing movement and snuffling sounds coming from the crib. It wasn't long before Melanie was crying loudly.

Lauren pushed herself out of Rick's arms. "I'm sorry. I guess I woke her." She wiped ineffectually at her wet eyes with her fingers before spying a box of kleenex on the kitchen bench and snatching a handful.

Rick quickly crossed the room to the crib. "I don't think it was you," he said as he picked up Melanie. "The nanny who came with me as far as St. Thomas Airport said I could expect some problems. She warned me Melanie was teething. And I was up to her half a dozen times last night. It looks like tonight will be a repeat performance."

"May I?" she asked as she stepped closer to Rick and held out her hands to the baby.

He relinquished Melanie to Lauren's arms and swallowed a lump in his throat. Lauren moved across to the sofa and sat down, holding the child close.

"I'll just find the teething gel," Rick said huskily.

Lauren held Melanie against her chest and crooned soft words against the baby's ear while tears streamed down her face. Rick sat down next to them with his arm resting around Lauren's shoulders. He blinked a suspicious tingle away from his eyes.

Lauren was lost in a world of her own. He had no doubt she was imagining the child was hers, if only for this small piece of time. He hoped he was doing the right thing in allowing Lauren to continue holding Melanie. He wasn't sure, but he guessed it could only do her good to expel the grief.

Eventually, Lauren noticed Melanie was still crying. "I think she's joining me in sympathy," she said with a watery smile.

"Here's the gel. Would you like to hang on to her while I put it on her gums?"

"Okay," she sniffed.

Rick smiled grimly while he spread the clear gel over Melanie's gums. It was difficult, partly because the baby was chewing on his fingers at the same time, but mainly because it brought him in close proximity to Lauren. His body was besieged with a strange mixture of compassion and yearning. He had never felt so powerless in his life.

In the boardroom, he was in his element. There, the cut and thrust of financial negotiations fulfilled his passion for being in control of his environment. Nothing, not even the diplomacy required to solve the day-to-day issues of aged care, had prepared him in any way for Lauren.

When Melanie continued to cry, despite the gel, Rick took her from Lauren and started to pace the room.

Lauren said, "I know someone who takes her baby for a drive in the car every evening to get him to sleep. You never know, a walk in the stroller could work just as well."

Rick kept pacing, jiggling Melanie in his arms and looking increasingly flustered. "You could be right. All I know is, I have to do something. She'll disturb everyone in the whole resort, the way she's going."

Lauren smiled to herself, relieved to diffuse the tension in her body. The unflappable Rick was not so unflappable after all. "I assume you have her stroller?"

The crying bout must have been just what she needed, Lauren suddenly felt as if a great weight had lifted from her body. She suppressed more laughter when Rick slid his fingers through his hair for the hundredth time in the last five minutes. His neatly groomed style was looking distinctly ruffled.

"Yes. Yes. Over there."

After a few more fraught minutes, the stroller was assembled and Melanie settled amongst a snug bundle of baby blankets. Rick lifted the stroller down the porch steps and they headed quickly up the path that led away from the resort and the other guests.

The stroller trundled over the uneven ground in the pool of light Rick aimed just in front of them. They walked in companionable silence, the jolt of the stroller over pebbles and sticks strewn on the unpaved path quickly lulling Melanie to sleep. By the time they had traveled twenty yards along the nature trail, she was out like a light.

"I think we should stop for a minute," said Rick. "I expect the trail will be a bit too rough for the stroller a bit further up. We can sit on this boulder and wait a while before we go back, in case Mel wakes again."

Lauren sat next to Rick on the smooth rock. It was rough and cool beneath her hand. The fine hairs on his arm brushed against hers and the zing of an electric current scattered any thoughts of a comfortable silence. She tensed her fingers, scraping her nails on the rock. Her heartbeat drummed in her ears and she swallowed the tension mounting in her body.

But this was nothing like the tension that preceded a panic attack. This was... electric. I don't want this, she screamed in her mind. I won't make a fool of myself. Not again.

"Could you turn the flashlight off," she said suddenly. "I want to feel the tranquility. Don't you love the peace and quiet?" She knew she was babbling but the tension in her body begged for release and she was terrified her runaway thoughts were written all over her face.

"You call this quiet? It's rowdier than Annaberg market."

"Maybe. But it's different. Listen."

Rick snapped the light off. They didn't speak for several minutes. Lauren did relax then. She let the cacophony of night noises gradually separate into individual sounds of wildlife and native birds.

Lauren turned and opened her mouth to speak. Her breath locked in her throat as she encountered Rick's face, mere inches from her own, barely discernible in the faint moonlight filtering through the trees. Whatever words she may have voiced dried in her mouth. Everything slowed. Seconds became minutes. She almost forgot to breathe. She imagined Rick's mouth on hers again. She remembered the hard heat of his lips; the way his soft hair had felt feathering through her fingers and the hard-packed muscles of his stomach and chest.

She remembered the kiss. She wanted a repeat of that exquisite pressure on her mouth. Now. Pure desire took over every other thought process.

She leaned toward him, silently begging for his mouth on hers. She stared into his hooded eyes; her own flickered down to his lips.

"Don't you ever wait to be asked?" he whispered without rancor.

Lauren swallowed. "I... I..." Her eyes fluttered closed as Rick's head descended and covered her mouth.

His hand rested lightly on her knee. The heat of it burned into her skin. She shifted on the hard rock as she felt a sudden throbbing awareness deep inside her.

"Lauren," Rick murmured against her mouth. His tongue traced a searing trail along her bottom lip before his teeth nibbled gently.

She sucked in her breath and leaned into his body, oblivious to anything except the riotous feelings surging along her veins. They were wrapped in a cocoon of thick velvet blackness. The tropical forest surrounding them obliterated most of the stars and it was easy to imagine the rest of the world existed only in dreams. They were alone except for the sleeping child.

Rick's fingers traced the warm skin of her arm, searing it with an electric current and making the fine hairs spring up. When he reached her shoulders, he gently cupped them in each palm while his mouth left hers and moved down her neck to her collarbone leaving tiny butterfly kisses in his wake.

Lauren threw her head back and scooped in the oxygen that had been lacking up until then. She tried not to think. For a fleeting moment, Brian's condemning face flitted into her consciousness, but she swept it away. Rick was not Brian, she reminded herself. *This* was nothing like Brian.

Rick's fingers found and released the tie at the nape of her neck. The fabric dropped to her waist. She should have blushed. Would have, if it had been daylight. As it was, he couldn't see her, any more than she could see him. She knew this had to be wrong, but she couldn't hold the thought.

She was riding a magical wave of discovery. She could feel his fingers and his lips. She could smell the delicious scent of him mingled with the freshness of the ocean. She could sense the restrained power of him under her own fingers as they dug into the rippling muscles of his back.

He had yet to touch her bare breasts, but she could feel the burgeoning of her nipples. They tightened in anticipation. The warm night air caressed her skin and she waited for his touch.

At last she felt the hot wetness of his mouth. It was nothing like she expected. Her whole body burst into flame. The breath left her lungs in a whoosh and her bones turned to liquid fire. She whimpered and clung to him. She squeezed her eyes shut.

"Rick," she sobbed, unable to get any other word out.

She felt his hot mouth on her breast and she was swept up in a tumultuous wave of longing. Wanting. The only lucid thought was an overwhelming need to be held closer and closer.

Somehow they slid to the ground. Lauren had no idea how she had got there. It was only when Rick pulled her against him to shield her back from the rough ground that she registered their change of position.

She was lost, adrift on a sea of pure sensation. The

only thing that mattered or had any relevance was Rick's magic touch. A man she had known such a short time. And yet, was that really true? She had heard of soul mates. Souls that had known each other again and again in past lives. People that were drawn together without either fully understanding why.

These thoughts floated in and out of her mind, but they, like everything that was happening to her, took on the quality of gossamer. Thoughts that this should not be happening came and went without ever taking root.

Rick's lips returned to hers and they kissed like Lauren had never imagined a kiss could be. They drank of each other's very essence. She never wanted it to end. It had to go on and on. It must, for if he stopped now, she would surely die.

The words *I love you* burst into her brain, but were quickly subdued. It's too soon, don't trust your feelings, came the futile warning of sanity.

Her fingers reached for the buttons on his shirt. She released each one and sighed with delight when his chest and stomach were free for her to revel in. She touched. She licked. She kissed. She savored.

While her hot cheek glided over his hard stomach and she inhaled his masculine scent, Rick slid his fingers inside her shorts and over her fanny.

"Oh, Lauren, honey. You're so beautiful." She barely recognized the husky voice, but thrilled with the knowledge that his desire for her was as much out of control as hers was for him.

She could feel his hands on her skin, his mouth on her lips. But the kiss was not enough. Not even close. She wanted more. Her body demanded more. This was never going to be enough.

"Rick, Rick," she sobbed. "I..." But the words

wouldn't come. Her brain had stopped functioning, except on the most elemental of levels.

He kissed her closed eyes gently. "I want to take away all your pain," he whispered. "And replace it with your *heart's desire*."

She felt his hardness against her stomach and experienced a primal surge of power. Her hand moved instinctively. He gasped, and then groaned into her neck. They were both swept along on a tide of pure sensuality. Lauren didn't want it to end. Ever.

Suddenly, Rick gently removed her hand from his hardness. "Honey, we can't. Not... now. Not here."

She almost cried out in anguish. He couldn't stop now!

He held her close as she buried her face in his bare chest.

All of a sudden she registered her own near nakedness and started to pull away.

He tried to stop her. "Don't run away," he said huskily.

She covered her breasts with her hands. Embarrassed heat flooded her face and she was thankful for the darkness. "Someone might come," she said desperately as she dragged up the fabric over her breasts.

"My point exactly," he said wryly.

The full implication of their situation suddenly hit home, leaving her mortified. She fumbled for the ties that would put her halter top back into place, but her hands shook, making the task impossible.

"Here. Let me," said Rick gently.

She sat rigid while his warm hands moved over her trembling fingers. He fumbled with the ties then eventually completed the job, gathering her into his arms.

She resisted him at first, but gave in when he whispered. "I just want to hold you. That's all."

And she wanted to be held. Despite still feeling light-headed and disoriented, she wanted nothing more than to be in his strong arms.

He kept her against him in an iron grip and kissed her hair. After a while, some of the embarrassment faded, yet she still didn't trust her voice.

Eventually, it was Rick who spoke. "I'm trying to find the right words but none that come to mind seem adequate. I don't know what happened."

She swallowed and said nothing.

"It felt right," he said.

"Yes," she whispered. He did understand.

"But it wasn't right. It shouldn't have happened. I hardly know you."

Her heart dropped like a stone. If she'd been punched in the stomach she couldn't have felt worse.

"I don't think you are ready for this either," he continued.

She felt the sting of tears in her eyes but she willed them away.

"You're on the rebound from Brian and... you're still grieving for your baby."

"No. Rick..."

He touched her lips, silencing her words. "Don't say anything. What you feel for me...it's not real —"

Lauren launched herself out of his arms. She was mortified. How dare he cheapen what had happened between them!

"You arrogant... toad! Where do you get off presuming to understand me, or my feelings? If you don't want to make love with me – just say so! But, for your information, I have no intention of making love with you, let alone falling in love with you. Now or ever! Put that in your patronizing pipe and smoke it." She turned and ran down the path, barely noticing when she tripped and fell.

She scrambled back up before Rick realized and came to her rescue.

The tears were streaming down her face. How she made it back to her villa she never knew. She was only aware of one thing. She felt utterly humiliated. She would never be able to face him in the morning. Right now, she wished herself a million miles away.

Five

THE next morning, Lauren lay in bed a long time after the stripy dawn light filtering through the shutters had woken her from a restless sleep. She stared at the exposed timber ceiling and listened to the early morning sounds of the island's bird-life. The plaintive calls no longer sounded sinister and she wondered how she could have ever confused them with a baby. Melanie's cry sounded nothing like them.

She blocked out thoughts of the child and instead, re-played all of the previous evening's embarrassing events in her mind. Perhaps by doing so, she could put the whole humiliating saga into perspective. She quickly realized her mistake in dwelling on the memories when she remembered what it felt like to be molded into Rick's wickedly sexy body.

She recalled with unnerving clarity the way her skin had tingled every time he touched her. Her stomach fluttered crazily all over again. How she wished she could block the vivid memory of his mouth on hers. But she couldn't shake the potent vision. She could feel his hot, searching tongue as if he were in bed with her right now. She could almost smell his delicious scent, a mixture of tangy aftershave and something else potently male. It drugged her senses and fuzzed her brain. She shook off the dangerous memory. She hated the control he had over her body, even in her imagination.

She sighed and acknowledged the fickleness of her emotions with a kind of sick resignation. She didn't want Rick to make her feel this way, but another part of her reveled in the hot surge of desire that assailed her whenever she re-lived the memory of his touch.

The feelings were only physical, of course. Lust, pure and simple. She wasn't silly enough to get carried away imagining any finer feelings; her determination not to risk her heart again made sure of that. But still... No sense in playing with fire. She mustn't forget the baby. If it was only the possibility of falling for Rick she had to fear, she'd have no concerns, but Melanie was another matter. She could imagine herself growing attached to the sweet child without any difficulty at all and for that reason she had to keep her wits about her.

If Rick had been on the island alone, she may have considered a night of hot sex. She laughed at her wild thoughts. Maybe she would, maybe she wouldn't, she amended, but it would have been delicious to explore the possibilities. Even if it was only in her imagination! She could prove to herself once and for all she was ready to take on life with as much fun and gusto as possible.

Things had been progressing well before Rick had arrived. She'd been having a ball and had almost succeeded in forgetting her problems. Sure, there hadn't been anyone she'd been tempted to experiment with until Rick had burst on the scene, but that didn't mean a diabolically sexy guy hadn't been just around the corner.

Someone like Rick.

She swept the sheet back and swung her legs off the bed. Her fantasies were getting away from her. Attracted to Rick or not, she was treading on dangerous ground indulging in them. Far safer to avoid thinking about him and concentrate on enjoying her vacation without the sexy daydreams. Yes, she told herself firmly, best you keep well away from him.

She picked up her wristwatch from the bedside table

and noted it was getting late. She'd have to hurry if she expected to have breakfast and still leave enough time to catch the morning ferry to St Thomas. She had made up her mind to take one of the island tours. And she was suddenly starving.

Lauren eyed Rick's villa when she skipped down the stairs fifteen minutes later and a swarm of insane bees buzzed in her stomach. She relaxed slightly when she saw no sign of movement and didn't hear any sound coming from the villa.

She let out the breath she had been holding and walked down the leaf-strewn path, padding rapidly along in her sandals. She had her swimsuit, towel, sunscreen and purse in a string bag slung over her shoulder. Her eyes were shaded with a straw hat and sunglasses. Anyone observing her would have seen a woman without a care in the world, enjoying her vacation and looking forward to the coming day. And she was. Or she would be, once she was certain Rick wasn't about to spring from the undergrowth at any moment.

The restaurant was nearly empty when she reached the door. She collected her usual plate of fresh fruit and a cup of steaming coffee and took it out to the terrace. She slid a slice of mango into her mouth and reveled in the delicious explosion of sweet soft fruit on her taste buds. She closed her eyes.

This is the life...It would be warmer today, she reflected as she reached for another piece of fruit. There was no breeze and already the sun shone hot on the bare skin of her arms.

"May I join you?"

Lauren almost jumped out of her skin as the deep voice broke through her reverie. She coughed as a piece of watermelon nearly went down the wrong way.

A warm hand patted her on the back. "Sorry to startle you."

Lauren looked up at the tall figure and almost laughed aloud when she saw it was Lars, one of the yacht owners. He was well over six foot, with white-blond hair and piercing blue eyes. He was the classic beach boy image and no doubt had his pick of women. She felt none of the zing of awareness she felt with Rick, and she was glad.

"Lars! Hi! Yes, yes, please sit down." She was so relieved it wasn't Rick, her invitation was enthusiastic and warm.

"Thanks," he grinned as he slid into the chair beside hers. "I don't often see you alone."

She bit her lip. "No, um..."

"It's okay. No need to explain." His eyes crinkled at the corners and his teeth shone white in the sun. "I was just surprised. That uptight looking guy seems to have the hots for you. Managed to avoid him this morning, hey?"

Lauren blushed. "He's not — I'm not —"

Lars chuckled. "Forget I mentioned him. Got any plans?"

Lauren was relieved. The last person she wanted to discuss was Rick. "I was thinking of taking a day trip out to the one of the islands."

"Great. So was —"

Suddenly their conversation was interrupted by the sound of loud, animated talking. They both turned and saw four people heading for their table.

Bob, one of the yacht owners, slapped Lars on the back. "Morning, bro. Hope we're not interrupting anything." He chuckled, winked at Lauren and promptly sat down beside Lars.

Maureen, his wife, added her soft trilling laugh.

ANDREA FULLER

"Honey, Lars might not want us here. He and Lauren didn't look like they were expecting company."

"Course he wants our company. Don't you, Lars?"

Lars grinned at Lauren. He looked back at Bob and shrugged. "Have a seat, since you already have."

"Told you." Bob grinned at his wife.

She gave him a withering look but didn't protest further.

Mitch and Sue joined them as well and soon the six of them were enjoying breakfast together. Lauren was relieved and happy the group had turned up. She was starting to recapture the way she had felt right up until Rick had entered the scene two nights ago. She was amongst friends. Casual and passing, yes, but non-threatening and fun to be with.

She was disappointed to hear that Bob and Mitch and their wives were leaving that morning to continue their cruise. They expressed disappointment that Lauren couldn't come with them to Sage Island National Park. The area was famous for its caves and they planned to spend the day there. They didn't intend to return to St. John afterwards so couldn't offer to take Lauren with them.

"No problem," chimed in Lars. "I've got no plans for the next few days that can't be broken. I'll keep her entertained." He winked at Lauren and she smiled back tentatively. She felt a frisson of nervousness skitter down her spine at his presumption. Having no intention of diving headlong into yet another relationship, she shook off the feeling. She was being silly. Lars was harmless. He was just being friendly and she did need some fun to get her mind off Rick and Melanie.

She felt a brush on her shoulder and turned abruptly, frowning at the sharp intrusion into her thoughts. A tall figure shadowed the sun and she had to blink before she could focus.

"Rick," she whispered, greeted with the unreal sensation of having conjured him up from her daydreams. At least he was alone.

"Please excuse the intrusion, Lauren. May I speak to you, please?"

She swallowed having suddenly found it impossible to answer with her mouth devoid of moisture. "I... I don't think so," she replied. She nibbled on her bottom lip. "I mean, not right now. Maybe later."

Rick looked uncomfortable and Lauren suddenly felt sorry for him.

"Is this guy giving you trouble, Lauren?"

Lars looked about ready to punch Rick on the nose and Lauren was tempted to giggle at the bizarre situation. Was it only hours ago that Rick had warned her about the man who was now all geared up to protect her?

She was about to reassure Lars his over-protectiveness was totally unnecessary, when Rick cut in. "Lauren is a friend of mine," he said pompously.

Lars stood up. "Is that so? She doesn't look too keen to see you."

Lauren, seeing the situation about to escalate out of control, stood also. "It's okay, Lars. Rick, please. I'll see you later. We can talk then."

He looked about to argue, but said, "Fine. Later then."

Rick walked away and Lauren watched him go with a sinking heart. She felt mean, at a loss. She had no time to dwell on her uncomfortable feelings, as Bob stood up as well. "We're off," he announced when the others followed suit.

"So are we, if we're going to catch the water taxi," announced Lars. "Coming, Lauren?"

"I hadn't totally decided," she began.

"You can't miss seeing Great Thatch Island. We can go snorkeling or scuba diving or even see the coral through a submarine."

She glanced in the direction that Rick had gone.

"Come on," he coaxed. "We'll have a great time."

She turned back to him. "Okay," she smiled. She did want to see the island and if she stayed behind she'd only spend the day trying to avoid Rick and her vacation would be spoiled again.

"Great! Let's go."

They walked the short distance down to the dock to the waiting water taxi. There were two other couples waiting, and after everyone was aboard there was a shout from the dock. A last minute passenger headed toward them.

Lauren turned and her heart sank. It was Rick. And Melanie.

"Just in time," commented the skipper when Rick reached them.

Rick, a bag hooked over one arm, stepped aboard, clutching Melanie on his hip. He took the last space on the bench seat next to Lauren. The only way she could keep her distance from him was to move closer to Lars. Even so, when Rick sat down with Melanie on his knee, Lauren found herself pressed against his arm.

"Where are you off to?" Lars asked Rick.

"Same place as you, of course." Rick was abrupt.

"You're not taking Melanie out to Johnson Reef, surely!" blurted Lauren before she could stop herself.

"I'm not going to the reef. I'm only getting a lift as far as Leinster Bay," he answered blandly.

"Oh," was all she could manage in reply.

"I'm going shopping in Annaberg," he added. "I've got a few things to get for Melanie."

"Oh," she said again. She looked at Melanie and the baby gurgled. She couldn't help grinning at the happy child. Suddenly, a sweet image of Rick taking Melanie shopping planted itself on her mind. She looked up into Rick's face and her heart contracted. His expression was implacable. Her smile disappeared. What had she done wrong?

Lars slipped his arm around her shoulders and helped her get comfortable. She tried to convince herself it was just to make more room for her but Rick was glaring again. Coral Bay couldn't come quick enough.

"Won't it be a bit awkward shopping with a baby?" she asked, mainly to distract Rick from Lars' hand stroking her shoulder. She wanted to shrug it off but not while under Rick's scrutiny.

"I'll manage."

"Couldn't Cathy have looked after Melanie for you?"

"Not all day. No."

"I —"

"I was going to ask you to come with us," he said before she could speak. "I was hoping you could help me." She couldn't miss the censure in his voice.

"I'm sorry. I didn't know. And I promised Lars," she said in a small voice.

Rick saw the guilt in Lauren's eyes and regretted his comment and the tone. He didn't want to hurt her but hell, she was hurting him. He felt sick at the sight of Lars' possessive grasp on her. It took all of his self-control not to thump the man and throw him overboard. He wanted to pulverize the man's face and feed him to the sharks.

He couldn't help remembering the feel of Lauren in his arms the night before. He was certain he hadn't imagined her response to him. He'd been in a daze at his own reaction to her closeness but not so muddle-headed that he wasn't sure the feelings were mutual. And yet, here she was, cozy with this Neanderthal. Well, it just proved he was right about her after all.

To think he had been feeling guilty for his initial judgment of her. Her tantalizing body and evocative scent must have scrambled his brain. Not to mention the effect her soft lips and delectable face had on his sanity.

He clenched his teeth. The woman was a witch. No doubt about it, he must be mad to be sitting here next to her. He hadn't lied. He was going shopping at Annaberg, but he'd originally intended to catch the afternoon ferry, until he'd seen her and Lars heading down the beach to the waiting water taxi. Maybe he'd catch a flight back to Miami and call Janice.

He re-settled Melanie on his knee when she twisted around trying to reach Lauren. Who was he kidding? He had no intention of leaving St. John as long as Lauren was there. As much as he knew it was an exercise in stupidity, he couldn't seem to help himself. In fact he felt all at sea at the way his life, once so neat and orderly, had obtained the amazing ability of unraveling with break-neck speed.

He sighed. Once Janice had sorted out whatever was keeping her away, everything would be fine. He'd put his life back into order again and Lauren would become a frustrating, yet rather pleasant, memory.

He stared toward Leinster Bay, which was thankfully getting closer with every passing minute.

When they finally arrived at the harbor, he crossed the gangplank and walked up the jetty without so much as a backward glance at Lauren and Lars. He didn't think his stomach could stand another look at the two of them cuddled up together. He felt sick to his boots at the fool he had made of himself. Lauren must be laughing her head off at him. In fact, he was starting to doubt now whether her reaction to him had been as spontaneous as he had thought at the time.

What did he know about women anyway? Maybe she'd been laughing at him all along. With his track record he ought to have known better than to trust his instincts. A woman had already made a fool of him once. Lauren made it number two.

He shrugged off his foolishness, grasping onto his building anger instead. Well, good luck to her if she wanted to prey on stupid fools like him. At least he hadn't lost his heart to her. She was a sexy eyeful and she would have fooled any man. Out of sight, out of mind was going to be the order of the day.

He headed for the stores and tried to blank her from his mind.

Lauren was trying to ignore Rick while clamping down the urge to run after him. She allowed Lars to steer her to the office where they would buy their tickets for the reef trip. Once they were aboard the catamaran heading out past the islands to Johnson's Reef, she felt better. Well, safer from the insidious temptation of Rick, anyway.

The trip out to the reef was rougher than she expected but she avoided seasickness, having taken the medication recommended by the cabin crew. It took two and a half hours to get there after stopping at Whistling Cay to pick up more passengers.

The sky was a brilliant blue, the sea a deep emerald green shot with silver flecks from the sun. She was fascinated by the myriad of tiny islands they passed, some little more than jagged rocky outcrops or a clump of trees growing on a strip of sand. Some of the islands could have been walked around in less than ten or twenty minutes. A few had small boats moored near the beach or in deep inlets that formed secluded bays where yachts moored overnight.

Lauren sat with Lars outside on the bow, soaking up the fresh breeze as the catamaran sliced through the waves leaving salty spray in its wake.

A couple of times she imagined it was Rick sitting next to her. But she quickly berated herself and returned her full attention to the passing islands.

Finally they reached Coral Bay Reef and the catamaran pulled up beside a floating pontoon. Before leaving the boat they enjoyed the delicious seafood buffet of fresh shrimp, calamari, oysters and tropical salads. While they ate, the cabin crew gave the passengers directions on the various ways of viewing the reef. Lauren opted to check out the underwater viewing room with four walls of windows to admire the colorful fish and coral. They then agreed to snorkel and Lars came with her, even though she knew he could scuba dive.

From the moment she dipped her face into the warm tropical waters of Coral Bay she was transported to another world. She was floating on the surface of the water but the sounds above her disappeared and all she could hear was the sound of her own rhythmic breathing. A myriad of fish of all sizes darted in and out of the coral, seaweed, clams and sea anemone.

By the time they were on their way back across the sea through the islands Lauren was relaxed, sun-kissed and pleasantly exhausted.

As they approached the wharf, Lauren saw Rick and Melanie standing on the dock. Her heart leapt. He was waiting for her. She couldn't wait to tell him all about her day. How she wished he had been with her. Then common sense reasserted itself. What was she thinking? Too much sun, she berated herself. But she couldn't help the little skitter of anticipation at the thought of seeing Rick again.

Lars helped her from the catamaran but she hardly noticed; she was too busy looking over to where Rick had been standing. But he had gone. She felt disappointed and that made her annoyed with herself.

She walked back to the beach with Lars then said with false brightness, "Thanks for a lovely day, Lars. I had a wonderful time."

"I'm glad," he smiled. "How about dinner on my yacht?"

"Oh! I don't know. I'm really tired..."

He smiled disarmingly. "I won't keep you late and I'm leaving tomorrow. It would mean a lot to me to spend my last night on St. John with you."

Lauren glanced involuntarily over to the empty beach. "Okay. That would be lovely but I have to shower and change first."

Lars looked at his watch. "That's fine. I have some things to do on my yacht anyway. How about I meet you back here at six and I'll take you across in the dinghy."

"Right. I'll see you then."

Lauren found it hard to get excited at the prospect of an evening alone with Lars as she dressed in her sarong and short t-shirt. Lars was loads of fun and a perfect gentleman, but she found herself missing that spark of something extra she experienced when she was with Rick.

She wrinkled her nose. Rick is an insufferable man, she reminded herself, but she enjoyed arguing with him. It made her feel alive somehow. Still, Lars was pleasant and non-threatening. If she were sensible she'd accept he was just what she needed. She was better off without the heady mixture of excitement and confusion that seemed to invade her whenever Rick was around.

As promised, Lars was ready for her at six. He rowed them the short distance to his yacht just as the sun was setting, painting the horizon with slashes of purple, pink and orange. There was only one other boat anchored in the bay, but it was in darkness. Lars' yacht was well lit, as she clambered aboard, she noted he had the table set and a salad already prepared. Two steaks were marinating in a dish on the sink next to an open bottle of red wine.

"Would you like a glass of cabernet sauvignon while I cook our steaks?" he asked.

She looked around the neat compact boat and nodded. "That would be nice."

"Great. Have a seat then."

The red wine was a lovely way to relax after the tiring day on the reef and she savored its full-bodied taste. Over their perfectly cooked steaks they chatted. Lauren wouldn't be drawn about herself but Lars, who had been traveling around the world for several months, kept her entertained with amusing stories of his escapades. Some time later, she was surprised to watch Lars tip the last of a second bottle into their glasses.

"Goodness," she giggled. "I had no idea we'd drunk so much."

He chuckled. "Time flies when you're having fun."

She sighed and put down her dessertspoon after finishing the last mouthful of chocolate ice cream. "Thanks for a lovely evening, Lars," she smiled dreamily. She was feeling deliciously mellow.

"Thank you. I've enjoyed your company too. How about I clear these dishes while you make yourself more comfortable over on the divan."

She giggled. "You're not trying to seduce me are you? You naughty boy!"

"I'm offended! Don't you trust me?"

She kissed him softly on the cheek. "Of course I do. You've been a perfect gentleman. Thank you."

Lars drew her gently toward him when she went to move away. "You're a special lady, Lauren," he whispered before kissing her gently on the lips. "I don't want to spoil what we have together by rushing you. All in your time, my love."

His lips were soft and warm and rather pleasant. No sparks went off and no zing of desire spiraled through her body, but she was glad. It was nice to be with a man and not feel overwhelmed with unwanted desire. She could trust Lars and it made her relax further into his arms.

Lars brushed her lips lightly with his own then deepened the kiss. She pulled gently away and touched his lips with her finger in admonishment. "Now, now. That's enough for tonight," she smiled.

He frowned. "Come on, Lauren," he coaxed. "You can't stop now." He tried to kiss her again but she turned her head away.

"No, Lars."

He took her chin firmly in his hand and bowed his head toward her mouth. "You don't have to play hard to get," he growled. "I picked up your signals loud and clear. We both want the same thing."

"No, Lars," she said again with an edge of desperation in her voice. "I mean it!"

She realized now she'd had more wine than she should have. She heard her own voice slur and her limbs didn't want to obey her urgent commands. She felt sluggish and thick headed. Even so, she managed to evade his searching mouth and wriggle away from him.

"Lars, I want to go back to the resort. Now!"

He laughed. "But it's much more private here. No one can hear you scream," he growled with an attempt at sexy humor.

A frisson of anxiety snaked up her spine as she realized how isolated she was. The yacht was moored only about thirty yards from the shore but it was nearly midnight and she could hear the sound of music across the water coming from the restaurant. He was right. No one would hear her if she called for help.

She started to fight Lars in earnest as his hands and mouth seemed to be everywhere. She squirmed and tried to push him away, but his arms had her in an iron grip, his groping mouth leaving a wet trail over her face. When he started to paw at her breasts and attempted to push up her top, she fought him in earnest.

Finally, she wrenched herself from his grasp and raced up the steps toward the deck.

"Lauren!" he bellowed.

Blood pounded in her ears and she nearly tripped on the top step. She stumbled and regained her balance just as he caught her. She panicked and screamed. "No, Lars. Let me go! You're hurting me!"

He had hold of one wrist; it felt like a hot steel band digging into her tender flesh. His other arm was tight around her waist.

She kicked out with her high heels, feeling the connection with his shin. He yelped in pain and let go of her wrist. She took the opportunity to shove him again while he was off balance, then she was free. She ran across the deck. She didn't stop to think. She jumped straight over the side into the lagoon.

The water wasn't icy but it was still a shock. She had swallowed a mouthful before she regained her senses enough to tread water. She could still hear Lars bellowing at her and she imagined him jumping in and dragging her back onto the boat. The thought made her panic all over again and she started thrashing around in the water.

Her brain was still foggy from the effects of the wine and she couldn't think straight. The inky darkness of the water unnerved her. She couldn't orientate herself. She tried to tell herself to stay calm, but she was crying and thrashing at the same time.

Suddenly she felt the vice around her waist again. She screamed and kicked. "No! No! Leave me alone, Lars."

"Lauren!" The voice was urgent and pleading. "Lauren, it's me. Rick."

She immediately stopped struggling and burst into tears. "Oh Rick. Rick!" she sobbed as she wrapped herself around his body.

"Hey, careful. You'll drown us both. Stay still."

She did as she was told and allowed him to swim with her toward the shore. After a couple of minutes he whispered in her ear, "You can stand up now."

She did as he ordered and found the sandy bottom with her bare feet. Her shoes were gone and that made her start crying all over again.

Rick kissed her eyes and cheeks all the while murmuring soothing words. "It's okay, honey
. You're safe now."

When her legs refused to move, Rick scooped her up in his arms. "This is getting to be a habit," he whispered in her ear.

That made her cry all the harder. "I'm sorry, Rick."

Once they were on the beach he didn't put her down. Instead he took her straight to her villa and through to the bathroom.

"Are you right to undress yourself?" he asked gruffly.

A wave of embarrassment washed over her as she realized her short sarong and tiny tee shirt were plastered to her skin, outlining every curve of her body including her braless breasts.

She looked at Rick from under her eyelashes but he had averted his head. "Rick?"

"Yes?" he asked without turning.

"Thanks," she said tentatively.

"Don't mention it. Now, have a hot shower before you catch a chill."

She chewed on her lip. His voice was bland but she sensed he was angry with her. She opened her mouth to apologize again but quickly closed it and the bathroom door.

"I'm going over to my villa for a minute," he called from the other side of the door. "I just need to check on Melanie."

"Okay," she replied huskily.

He didn't answer. He was gone.

He hadn't returned half an hour later. She'd showered and dressed in Capri pants and baggy tee shirt then made herself a cup of tea. She tried to remember what he had said. She couldn't recall whether he had actually said he would return. She bit her lip. If he wasn't coming back, she should at least go over and apologize. If she waited until morning she was sure to have lost her nerve.

She padded across to Rick's villa and knocked softly on the door. She couldn't see any sign of life but there was a lamp spilling its soft light into the room.

"Hi. I was just on my way back to you."

Lauren jumped back, startled. Rick had come up the steps behind her. She glanced back at the open door of the villa. "But —"

"Cathy is inside."

"Oh." She bit her lip. The words of apology dried up on her tongue.

Rick gently brushed past her and stepped inside the door. Lauren wondered whether he expected her to follow but before she could make up her mind, he was back again with Cathy.

"Thanks again, Cathy," he smiled warmly.

"No problem! Goodnight, Rick. Lauren." She disappeared down the path and suddenly they were alone.

"I brought you these. I thought they might cheer you up." Rick offered her a small box.

"St. John chocolates!" Lauren looked at Rick's sheepish face.

"I'm glad you like them."

"I do."

For some reason the small gesture made her feel extraordinarily touched. He was maddeningly sexy and as irritating as a sleeping bag full of ants but he was also sweet and thoughtful. Her heart contracted and she felt the sting of tears in the back of her eyes.

"Thank you," she whispered when he didn't say anything more. She kissed him on the cheek. His skin was warm and alive. Her lips tingled.

"It's the least I can do after the fright you've had. What possessed you to go to that yacht, anyway?"

Lauren didn't hear the expected recrimination in Rick's voice and for once she wished he would rant and rave at her and call her all the stupid fool's under the sun. It was the least she deserved.

"I was stupid, I know. Lars hadn't given any hint he was interested in that way." Which wasn't quite true she admitted now, she had just decided to ignore the signals. But she wasn't about to tell Rick that. "I thought he just wanted to be friends."

"How could any man only want to be friends with you? Oh, hell. I didn't mean that the way it sounded."

"It's okay. I deserve it after the way I've been acting lately."

"I didn't mean— "

She touched his arm. "It is okay. Really. I just want to forget the whole horrible episode. I just came over to thank you for rescuing me. I... might have drowned if you hadn't been there," she finished in a whisper.

"I doubt that, but I'm glad you're okay. How about coffee to go with those chocolates?"

"If you don't mind, I think I'll go straight to bed." She blushed. "I mean —"

He cleared his throat. "I know what you mean. Goodnight then." He kissed her lightly on the mouth and as soon as he moved away again she felt bereft of his touch. She wanted him to take her into his arms.

"Goodnight," she whispered before going quickly down the steps and across to her villa.

At her door she turned. He was standing where she'd left him watching her intently. She lifted her hand in a half wave and dived into her villa before she gave into the urge to race back to him and throw herself into his arms.

Six

THE next morning, Lauren was sitting on the beach at Trunk Bay when the sun rose in its entire pink and orange splendor.

She found the unadulterated, fresh crispness of the new day uplifting and at once, a balm to her soul. The pure solitude allowed her to focus on herself, her life and her future. Here, in the freshness of a new morning, it was easier to be philosophical about the last few days.

Lauren had learned a lot about herself in the last six months. She had also come a long way in accepting the consequences of her impulsive nature. She could even admit that, as a teenager, she had often provoked her father.

Her counseling sessions had helped her to be brutally honest with herself. If she wanted to recover from post-traumatic stress, to go on to live a contented life, she had to accept certain truths. One of them was that avoiding your problems didn't solve anything.

She couldn't avoid the way Rick made her feel. She had known she was attracted to him, of course. She just hadn't realized how powerful that attraction could be. It seemed that every time he was near, she had no time to cope with her body's reactions. She was always carried along on a tide of sensation. When Rick had tried to gently let her down on a number of occasions, she had overreacted instead of taking it in her stride. She could even admit now, that rather than trying to hurt her, Rick was trying to tactfully save her feelings.

She hadn't actually blurted out those dreaded three

words. But she didn't need to, she guessed. She had revealed her deepest feelings in every caress of her hands, her lips, every moan and sigh.

She might be able to convince him he had been wrong that night on the nature trail – at least she hoped he had believed her vehement denials of love – but she wouldn't deny herself the sweet knowledge. Last night's fiasco had proven it was useless to hide from her feelings. Here, on the beach, where she had a moment separate from the rest of reality, she felt free to admit it. She had fallen in love with Rick. Not only Rick, but Melanie as well. In only days, her heart had been stolen away. Rather than experiencing dismay at the realization, she hugged the knowledge to herself and smiled.

Dreaming of a happy ending was pointless, she knew, but the very act of acknowledging her feelings was, in its own way, a releasing experience. She would have memories to keep and savor when she went home to Miami. Nothing could take that away from her.

She knew the three of them could never be a family. That daydream made her feel a bit of a fool, but the bittersweet secret of having two people to love in the privacy of her innermost heart gave her some comfort.

When the sun emerged over the horizon in its full glory, spilling sharp light into her shielded eyes, Lauren sighed deeply. She stood up, shrugged off her melancholy and walked briskly back to the path. Back to the real world.

She would cope. She was a fighter and nobody could take her own inner strength away from her.

"Where the hell have you been?"

Lauren's jaw dropped open. She was startled by the angry question flung at her and the glowering face of the speaker, as she emerged from the nature trail onto the main path leading back to the resort.

"Well?" Rick continued when she didn't answer despite snapping her jaw shut and then opening it again.

Her heart tumbled with tenderness at his unshaven face and delightfully messed hair, but none of her earlier thoughts showed on her face.

"Not that it's any of your business," she said calmly, "but I was watching the sun come up over Trunk Bay."

Some of the hot air seemed to expel from his heaving chest. "You should have told someone where you were going," he said with less heat. "What if something had happened to you?"

"Well it didn't," she said airily, knowing her flippant tone would annoy him, but scared of revealing her true feelings.

She repressed a small smile. He was absolutely gorgeous when he forgot to maintain his severe image. His hair was falling all over his forehead and his clothes looked like they'd been thrown on in five seconds flat. Melanie was perched on his hip, still wearing a stretch suit dotted with tiny teddy bears. Her hair was also pointing every which way and her wide eyes appeared to be taking in every word.

"What if something happened to you while you were alone?"

She blinked. There was no doubting the man was genuinely concerned for her. It thrilled her even as she tried to squash the bud of hope.

"You'd probably have heard me scream all the way to St Thomas, that's what!" She tried to sound indignant and fiercely resentful of his high-handedness, but Melanie was clutching Rick's shirt, blowing raspberries at no one in particular, and making it hard to concentrate.

The corner of Rick's mouth twitched when Lauren shifted her attention to Melanie and grinned at the child.

"That'd be nothing compared to the bellow I expect when I tan your backside for your stupidity," he said dangerously.

She stood her ground as Rick took two steps toward her. His anger seemed to have evaporated. Even the reluctant smile had gone.

"That thought does have possibilities," she said softly as her mouth dried to the texture of sun-bleached silk.

"You're doing it again." The rough timbre of his voice caressed the air around her.

"What am I doing?" she whispered, licking dry lips.

She watched him swallow and her lips parted.

"Flirting."

"I thought we'd gotten past that," she said cheekily. Stupid!

His eyelids fluttered down and up again in slow motion. The raucous sound of the island birds suddenly fell silent to her ears. She forgot about the baby. She forgot about everything else except the moment.

"I didn't mean to upset you when I... when we..."

"I know," she breathed.

"On the contrary, I enjoyed myself very... much," he husked. "I wasn't ready for you to leave last night."

"Now who's flirting?" Her voice came out as the barest of sounds.

"Rick! Rick!" called the now familiar voice of Cathy.

"Shoot," muttered Rick.

Lauren turned away as Cathy burst into view.

"Oh, Rick, there you are. Sorry to interrupt, but you're wanted on the phone."

Rick swallowed his frustration. He shrugged apologetically to Lauren before turning and hurrying toward the resort office.

He clutched Melanie to his chest and cursed the ill-timed intrusion. He had so much wanted to talk to Lauren about the night before last on the nature trail. He had made a total hash of it and he'd wanted to explain. Last night hadn't been the right time. But, this morning, he'd been determined to be honest with her about his feelings.

When he'd found her villa empty and then discovered she had missed breakfast, any logical thought had been impossible. Despite knowing his fears were irrational, he had imagined the worst. The sickness in his gut he had experienced when he had seen her jump over the side of the yacht had come back with wrenching intensity.

His thoughts were still full of Lauren and the way she always seemed to be able to rattle him as he picked up the telephone receiver from the office desk. He hoped this was Janice or Carl ringing to tell him they were on their way.

"Rick Masters," he rapped out.

"Mr. Masters, thank goodness!"

He suppressed a groan of annoyance at his secretary's voice. She had been in the job three weeks and was prone to the melodramatic. He'd left instructions with his Assistant Manager, Paul Baker, covering anything that might arise in the few days he'd expected to be away. But if something out of the ordinary had occurred, he had every confidence in Paul's ability to handle it.

"What is it, Fiona?" he asked with more tolerance than he was feeling.

"Everything! The auditors will be here in an hour and Mrs. Thompson's lawyer is insisting that if we don't do something about the retaining wall above her unit he'll sue us. And... and Pat said the flight times on her plane ticket are wrong and —"

"Fiona."

"— the computer people called and asked if we could put off next week's meeting another few days because their software expert can't make it —"

"Fiona!"

Silence. "Sorry, Mr. Masters. I... I just don't know what to do!" She promptly burst into tears.

Rick took two deep breaths before he felt able to speak without losing his temper. "Where is Paul?"

"Oh, I forgot to say that. His wife went into labor an hour ago and –"

"She's not due for another two months."

"I know. That's just it. They had to take her in an ambulance and Paul ran out of here, right in the middle of a meeting with —"

"Okay, okay, I get the picture. Book me on the afternoon flight out of St. Thomas. The water taxi leaves here at ten, so any flight after twelve will do."

"But, which airline should I call? I don't know what I've done with your itinerary." Her voice cracked in another sob and Rick bit down his mounting anger. He decided then and there the woman would be out on her ear the moment he got back to the office.

"Forget it. I'll arrange it from this end. Now, listen very carefully. Max can handle the auditors. As for Mrs. Thompson, I thought George was arranging for an engineer to check the cracks in the wall."

"I... I don't think he's had time..."

"Don't worry about that now. Call Mrs. Thompson's lawyer and set up a meeting with him at the site anytime that suits the day after tomorrow. And tell Pat she'll have to cancel her business meeting until everyone is back on deck. It wasn't urgent anyway. As for Netscope

Computers, having them defer doesn't worry me given the current situation, so you can call them back and tell them I'll speak to them tomorrow. Got all that?"

"Yes, Mr. Masters," Fiona said in a small voice.

"Good," Rick said before hanging up.

"Great. Just great!" he ground out. "And where the hell are Janice and Carl?" he added just for good measure.

He stared out of the office window at a cluster of tall palms. He would have to tell Lauren he was leaving. The thought left him cold. There was a lot of unfinished business between them. He had decided to stay on the island as long as Lauren was there, regardless of when Janice and Carl decided to turn up.

And Melanie. What would he do with her once he was back at work?

A half-formed idea began to take shape in his mind...

"No! Absolutely not!"

Rick's heart dropped. Hesitation he had expected. Excuses he could overcome. But he had not counted on Lauren's outright refusal. Of course he should have realized how she'd feel about it. He knew her background now. What had he been thinking? He was lost for words knowing there would be nothing he could say to change her mind. She was standing in front of him with her arms folded and every line in her body screamed rejection.

Lauren willed her heart to stop pounding in her ears. The dull thud made it hard to think. She needed to get away. She knew her tenuous control was fraying at the edges. She recognized her body's fear response.

She scooped air into her lungs and then tried to unobtrusively expel it slowly. She felt her palms dampen and her stomach churn.

It hurt that he had asked her to travel to Miami with him and act as nanny for Melanie. Was he that insensitive? Didn't he know his request would tear her apart?

Yet... in some other part of her brain she was tempted. No. Amend that. If things were different. If Melanie was his baby. If he cared for her. If she'd had any chance of a permanent relationship with him...

But wishing was futile. She had been foolish and fanciful this morning when she had imagined her love was enough. Ridiculous to think a glimpse at what might have been could sustain her throughout a lonely future.

She shook her head. It was time to get away from Rick. She needed time to think.

"Lauren?"

Her head swung around. She swallowed and eyed him warily.

"It's okay," he said. "I'm sorry. I shouldn't have asked. I just thought..." He grimaced. "It doesn't matter what I thought. It was insensitive of me."

Her face relaxed. She should have felt mean. But it was too much to ask. She searched for something, anything, to change the subject.

"When is the ferry leaving?"

For several seconds, Lauren thought Rick had not heard her. He was staring at her so strangely.

He seemed to shake off something. He glanced at his watch. "In an hour."

An hour.

In an hour he would be gone from her world forever. In an hour she could start working on the rest of her life.

"Would you like to chat while I pack?" he said.

Here was her escape. She didn't have to wait an hour. She could be rid of him now. *Just say no*.

"Yes. I'd like that."

She didn't need to dwell on her reasons. She knew the fanciful part of her didn't want to let him go just yet.

"I can spare an hour," she said.

He touched her cheek softly. "Good," he replied. "I'm glad."

They walked slowly to Rick's villa. Lauren's urge to flee had evaporated but her heart felt like a lead weight in her chest. Her eyes were stinging but she wouldn't cry. That would come later.

As soon as they reached the villa, Rick put Melanie on the bed and started to undress her.

"Can I?" Lauren asked uncertainly.

Rick looked around in surprise. He had thought Lauren was finding it too painful to have anything to do with the baby. This woman was still so much of an enigma.

"Sure. It'll save me some time. I'm afraid things are a bit of a mess. I'm not usually this disorganized," he said ruefully.

Lauren smiled to herself despite her heavy heart. She could just imagine Rick's home. All order and stark tidiness. Melanie would soon put paid to that!

She tackled Melanie's diaper while Rick started tossing things into an overnight bag.

"Any word from your elusive sister and her husband?" she queried casually. She knew she was mad to ask. That line of conversation was a veritable minefield, but she couldn't resist.

"No. It appears they're still delayed."

"So... what will you do? With Melanie. When you get to Miami, I mean."

Rick sighed. "I don't exactly know yet. I do have a neighbor who loves children. She has four grandchildren and they're often at her place so I'll try her first."

"I would have thought whatever is keeping Janice and Carl couldn't be more important than the welfare of a baby."

"I'm not sure what the problem is. I guess it must be important."

Something in Lauren snapped.

"Oh really?" she said sarcastically. "And, what, may I ask, is more important than a six month old baby?"

He didn't say anything for a while. "Janice took Kelsey's death hard."

His soft words did nothing to appease her anger. "All the more reason for her to come to Kelsey's daughter at the earliest opportunity."

He sighed. "I'm sure she will. When she feels ready."

Lauren scoffed. "And this is the woman who will be mother to Melanie? She sounds like a person who will take care of the baby's welfare when it suits *her*."

Rick finally lost control of his tightly reined feelings. "You know nothing of my sister and her problems. She and Kelsey were very close. She's found it hard to cope since... and she's had some problems with one of her teenage daughters. She has a lot on her plate."

"You don't, I suppose? And what about you? Has anyone given you a chance to grieve for your sister?"

"I'm fine," he said shortly.

"Ha. Typical male. Keep your feelings to yourself. Deny yourself the chance to be a human being!"

"Careful. You're treading on dangerous ground."

"Oh really! And what about your feelings for me?" she nearly shouted. All the pent up emotion and disappointment of losing him so soon, sprang from her body. "What about that?"

"Lauren —" he began in an anguished voice.

"You don't even care how I feel. You can brush me off

as if I were nothing more than a vacation fling —" She stopped. "Oh! That's it, isn't it? I was going to be nothing more than a quick —"

Rick closed the space between them. "Don't say it! Don't even think it. You mean more to me than that. Much more."

Lauren thrust Melanie at him and backed away. She didn't think she could cope with much more of this. She wanted to scream at him. If she meant so much to him, why was he leaving her? Surely work wasn't that important.

Her shoulders slumped. But of course it was. Her silly heart was getting way ahead of itself. Only this morning, she had been prepared to live without him. Was she so weak that she could fall to pieces so quickly? No.

"I'm sorry," she said when she reached the door, feeling blindly behind her for the catch. "I... I can't stay for a chat after all." She felt like laughing hysterically at the ridiculous words. She spun around and raced out of the villa and down to the beach.

Lauren sat on the sun-baked sand with her knees hunched up under her chin for a long time. It felt like forever but it must have been only twenty minutes.

She watched Rick walk up the beach toward the wharf and deposit his luggage on the dock. He handed Melanie to one of the resort staff before turning and strolling slowly back up to Lauren.

Involuntarily, she stood up and ran to meet him halfway. Now that the moment had come, she found she had to swallow a huge lump of clogged tears.

"Time to go," Rick said, his voice husky.

"Yes."

"Stay out of trouble, won't you," Rick said lightly.

"I never had a problem until you came along."

He eyed her curiously. She lowered her eyes and flushed. What a thing to say. She seemed to be making a career of inane comments, she reflected miserably.

"Or, if you can't stay out of trouble, at least try to reduce the damage," he smiled.

"Tone myself down, do you mean?"

He laughed. "If you like."

That hurt. After all the time they had spent together over the last two days, after everything that had happened between them, he still couldn't accept her the way she was. But, wasn't that just the point? He had all but admitted his future wife would be sedate, homely and predictable.

"I was just a challenge to you, wasn't I?" she managed bitterly while blinking frantically to prevent threatened tears from spilling.

"Excuse me?"

"You know. Challenge, as in someone who needed taking under your wing. Someone to reform."

His eyes softened at her strained words. He brushed lightly at the moisture squeezing at the corners of her eyes. "Lauren, I doubt whether anyone could change you. I certainly wouldn't want to try," he reproached. "You're perfect the way you are."

She said nothing. She couldn't. Her mind groped ahead to the moment when she could run to the safety of her villa and sob her heart out. She would allow herself that small indulgence before relegating him to a dark corner of her memory.

"I don't want us to part like this," he said quietly.

"No. I'm sorry. I... I've enjoyed your company over the last two days. And... Melanie is a delightful child."

He took a step toward her and looked at her uncertainly. She watched his eyes lower to her trembling lips before lifting again to her eyes.

"I hope everything works out," she said in a rush. "With your sister and... everything."

"Rick, you'll have to go or you'll miss the Sea Cat," someone called.

Rick turned and nodded to Jeff before facing Lauren again.

"I wish you would change your mind."

She stared into his face, searing every feature onto her memory. While the very air around them hushed and time hung suspended, she nearly said yes. The word hovered on her tongue. The pain of parting from him and the child was like a tangible thing. The effort of holding the choked tears in her chest almost overwhelmed her.

But if she gave into the agonizing temptation to stay with them, then wouldn't the pain of eventual parting be so much worse? To see Rick in his own home where her imagination would be let loose... no, she couldn't do it. She couldn't pretend to play "happy families" and then, when his sister finally turned up, calmly walk away. The very thought turned her blood to ice.

"It's too much to ask," she whispered through the tightness in her throat.

Rick felt his tenuous hold on hope slip through his fingers.

"Rick!" a voice called more urgently.

"I... I have to go. Can I call you?"

"I don't... think that would be a good idea."

Rick backed away, glancing toward the ferry in frustration then back at Lauren.

He dug a small piece of cardboard out of his pocket and shoved it into Lauren's palm. Then he gave her a quick, hard kiss. "Call me. Please," he said before turning and sprinting to the waiting ferry.

Lauren stared at the empty ocean for a long time after the ferry disappeared from view.

She pushed a strand of hair from her eyes and her fingers came away wet. She hadn't known she was crying.

"The contrariness of the female gender," she said flippantly to herself. She tried to laugh and dismiss the inexplicable feeling of loss as a temporary aberration.

Somehow the laugh rang hollow but she clamped down on her thoughts. Time enough later to dwell on every facial expression, every nuance of his voice, every touch... every kiss. For now, the grief was too raw and too painful to explore.

When the ferry disappeared from view with the two people she had lost forever, Lauren turned away from the beach.

Tomorrow she was going home to Miami. Just as well. There was nothing left for her here.

She finally looked at the crisp, white business card, now slightly crushed, in her palm. *Rick Masters. Managing Director. Corinella Aged Care Services.*

A tiny bud of hope flared in her chest. He still wanted to see her. Maybe... But, no.

She hadn't told him she could never have children.

She had only to remember the way his eyes softened when he looked at Melanie to know he was a man meant to have children of his own. He wouldn't marry a woman who could never bear him a child. And, even if he was prepared for the sacrifice, there was no way she could allow him to do it.

Seven

LAUREN'S heart pounded in her ears as the cab pulled up outside her father's house. Operating on autopilot, she paid the driver and climbed out of the car. She stood on the pavement, staring at the small weatherboard house that had been her home for twenty-five years. Countless memories came rushing back and she was powerless to stop them.

She could almost imagine her mother was still alive. She could be in the kitchen, preparing delicious treats as she had so often when Lauren was a child. She remembered how she had arrived home from school to the smell of hot pancakes dripping with melting butter and homemade strawberry jam...

She hadn't meant to come here, but she had found herself giving the cab driver her father's address instead of that of her friend, Tricia.

She had stayed with Tricia after the procedure. It was Tricia's parents who had insisted Lauren needed a vacation to complete her recovery and then surprised her with the airplane ticket to St. John.

By the time Lauren directed the driver to pull up outside number seventeen, she was a mass of nerves and uncertainties. She snatched up her bags and almost turned and headed for the phone box on the corner. Taking a deep breath, she dismissed the chaotic mixture of apprehension and lingering resentment and squared her shoulders. I can do anything, she reminded herself.

Once she was through the gate, it suddenly became easier. The dragging tension in her bones dissolved and was replaced with a resolute determination. At the front door, she knocked without hesitation. Almost immediately, the door swung open.

"Lauren!"

Lauren blinked at her father's unguarded reaction before the more familiar expression of stern blandness came over his face.

"Dad," she said with more calm than she was feeling. The handle of her suitcase dug into her clammy hand.

"Where have you been?"

Lauren bristled. *What do you care?* "On vacation."

"I called Tricia. She wouldn't tell me where you were. I was worried."

Worried? Frustrated that she was out of his control, Lauren amended for him bitterly. She shook her head. Maybe this wasn't such a good idea.

Suddenly she was enveloped in a bear hug. "Lauren, I'm... glad you're home." He pushed her away from him, looking sheepish before wiping his eyes with the back of his work-roughened hand.

Lauren blinked at her father's actions, so out of character for the cold man she remembered. It was six months since he had told her to never darken his door again. Could he have really changed that much?

"I'm not staying, Dad. I... I came to collect the rest of my things. I... I'm going back to Tricia's for a few days. Until I can find a place of my own."

"You can stay here," he said gruffly.

"I don't think so."

"But... Lauren, I'm so sorry about all those things I said when you..."

Memories hung heavily in the air between them.

"When I got pregnant, Dad. Can't you even say it?"

Her father cleared his throat. "Well, I *am* sorry. I

didn't realize how much until..." He opened the door wider. "We won't talk about that now. Come inside, darlin'. Won't you at least stay for dinner?"

"I can't..." As she watched her father's face fall, she swiftly made up her mind. "Okay, I'll stay for dinner. I guess it can't hurt," she added softly. She sighed and let her father pick up her bags. She followed him into the small living room at the front of the house.

She sat on the edge of the worn, floral brocade sofa and looked around the room. The wall-unit was crowded with photos; her parent's wedding photo, herself as a child, then a teenager and, later, her high-school graduation. An old piano sat in the corner, unused since her mother had become too ill to play. All the knick-knacks her mother had loved covered every polished surface in the room not already taken up with photos.

Lauren took in a deep, careful breath. "Mrs. Harris still cleaning for you, Dad?"

He scanned the room quickly before answering. "Yes. She does a good job, don't you think?"

"Yes."

Mrs. Harris had cleaned for them from when her mother had first been diagnosed with cancer. Nothing in the room had changed since that time. Except for the addition of photos of her teenage years by her father. It was six months since Lauren had been in this house, now she felt she had stepped back through a time warp to years earlier.

Strangely, she remembered the day her parents had gravely told her that her mother was very sick, more clearly than any memory since. She had been curled up in the chair reading a book, totally oblivious to the blow that was to come.

Nearly ten years later, she had been sitting up stiffly in

the same chair when she had told her father she was pregnant. She'd had to tell him alone. Brian had refused her his moral support.

"Would you like a coffee, darlin'? Or a sherry?"

Her father's unusually gentle words interrupted her painful memories. She turned to face him, blinking rapidly while she tried to re-focus on the present.

"A sherry would be nice. Sweet, if you have it."

He nodded and looked wistful for a moment. "Your mother liked sherry too."

"Yes."

"It helped with the pain a little at first. She found a glass or two relaxed her."

Lauren swallowed. "Yes."

"But it didn't help at all in the end."

She finally looked at her father properly. He was thinner than she remembered; his face had lost some of its harshness. He had deep lines and his skin was leathery from years of working outdoors. His hair was almost white; it had thinned considerably since she had last seen him. She suddenly realized he had aged. Her heart contracted painfully in her chest.

"I miss her too, Dad," Lauren said quietly.

Her father sighed and walked over to the buffet table where a glass decanter half-filled with a golden liquid stood on a silver tray with six upturned glasses.

"I loved your mother very much," he said with his back to her as he poured two glasses of sherry.

"I know, Dad."

"You remind me so much of her," he continued as he turned and handed her the glass.

Lauren took a sip of sherry, swallowing it with difficulty. As the warmth filled her throat then traveled down to her stomach, she stared at the worn, gray wool carpet, hardly daring to breathe.

She took another hasty sip before saying, "I shouldn't have blamed you for her death. It was irrational and unfair."

"It doesn't matter. You were only a child. You were hurting. We both were."

Nothing was said for a long time. When Lauren finished her drink, her father stood up and took the glass from her.

"Would you like another?"

Lauren laughed. "I'll end up rolling in the aisles. But, yes, I would like another."

Her father grinned and the tension evaporated. "I'll join you."

When they were each nursing a sherry again, Lauren slipped her shoes off and tucked up her feet.

"I want you to stay tonight, and for as long as you want," her father said suddenly. "Your old room is just as you left it."

Lauren looked at him. He had said he was sorry. He hadn't said he loved her, but he wasn't a man given to expressing his feelings. He looked at her expectantly and she saw the child-like hope in his eyes. It was enough.

"Yes, Dad. I'll stay."

His shoulders slumped and his face relaxed. He smiled. "Good, good," he said huskily. "I'll just put an extra steak on." He swallowed the last of his sherry and stood up.

Lauren suddenly felt light-headed and she knew the sherry had very little to do with it. She grinned and nearly gave in to the urge to throw her arms around her father.

She stood, placing her glass on the lamp-table beside the chair. She squeezed her father's hand and said, "I'll set the table." She couldn't say any more. The lump in her throat prevented it.

He nodded and his eyes were suspiciously bright as he went through to the kitchen.

It was while Lauren was taking the tablecloth and good cutlery from the buffet table that she heard a knock on the front door. For one ridiculous moment she imagined it was Rick coming for her. As soon as the thought came, she squashed it angrily. Just because things had taken a momentous turn for the better with her father, didn't mean she had to get carried away with further ridiculous possibilities.

"Could you get that, Lauren?" called her father from the kitchen where a delicious smell of sizzling steak wafted.

"Sure. Expecting anyone?" she called as she covered the short distance to the front door.

"Oh, I forgot to tell you," he replied. "It'll be..."

"Brian!" she gasped as she opened the door.

"Lauren!" He looked even more shocked than her father had been, if that was possible.

Lauren quickly recovered. "Brian, how are you?" she said with admirable calm.

"I... I'm great. How are you?"

Lauren's eyes shuttered as she recalled the last time she had seen him. She had been five months pregnant and had finally gotten up the nerve to tell him about the baby, unsure even then about his reaction. The revulsion that had come over his face when she had told him was indelibly imprinted onto her memory. She had hoped he'd be pleased. They had been intending to marry, after all. But he had reacted as if she'd suddenly grown two heads. She found it difficult now to assimilate that memory with the delighted surprise now displayed on his face.

"Have you come to see my father?" she asked politely.

He visibly shook himself. "Yes. We... er... have dinner

together every Friday night. We play chess," he added lamely.

"I see." Her voice was bland, but a riot of conflicting emotions vied for attention within her body. The one that over-rode all others was disappointment. She had been looking forward to a long talk with her father. She had a feeling that there were so many things they needed to say to each other.

Still blanking out any telltale expression from her face, she stepped away from the threshold and opened the door wide, beckoning for him to come in.

"Can I take those from you?" she indicated the brown bag containing two bottles of beer he was nursing under his arm.

Brian blinked several times. "Oh, yes. Thanks."

As Lauren led the way into the living room, the whole scene took on the quality of a weird dream. She felt herself detached from the situation. When her father came into the room, greeting Brian affably and glancing at Lauren with an apologetic look, she felt as if she were taking part in a play. Any minute the director would call "Cut!" and she would step away and back into the life she had known before that fateful knock on the door.

She was surprised to find dinner wasn't the ordeal she was expecting. She took part in the somewhat stilted conversation, thankful the news of her vacation tripped easily off her tongue. It was only when her father pleaded tiredness and declared he needed an early night that Lauren suddenly felt trapped.

She kissed her father's cool cheek and he squeezed her hand lightly before leaving and pulling the door closed after him. She turned back to the room and eyed Brian reclining comfortably on the sofa. For some reason she resented his obvious familiarity with her father's home. Her home, too, she reminded herself. Her father had welcomed her home and now, recognizing Brian appeared to consider himself part of it, she bristled.

"Can I get you coffee?" she offered.

"Perhaps, later," he replied confidently. "For now, I think we should talk." He patted the empty space next to him and Lauren bridled further at his presumption.

She remained standing. "Brian, I'm really very tired. Would you mind if we called it a night? I've been traveling most of the day and I think it's all caught up with me."

He leapt from the sofa, his face full of concern. "I'm sorry, sugar. How incredibly thoughtless of me. Of course I'll be going."

Lauren just stopped herself from breathing a heartfelt sigh of relief. Instead, she contented herself with a small smile. "Thanks for understanding, Brian. Perhaps we could have coffee sometime."

She was already walking to the front door, eager to be alone to sort through the emotion-fraught evening as well as being genuinely keen to get to bed. To her surprise, the comfort of her old room beckoned.

At the front door, Brian suddenly swept Lauren into his arms. Lauren was so shocked she stood rigid for several seconds until Brian released her.

"I'm sorry, Lauren, I shouldn't have done that. It's too soon."

She blinked. Too soon? What on earth was he talking about? This was the man who had rejected her. Cruelly and harshly. His next words gave her the answer.

"I made a mistake six months ago. A terrible, terrible mistake."

Lauren looked into his face and was genuinely shocked. The pompous confidence of a few minutes ago had disappeared. In its place was pleading uncertainty.

"It's okay," she said quietly. "I... I'm over it now. I've forgiven you and... and I think everything is going to be fine between Dad and me."

Brian sighed with relief. "That's great, Lauren. You have no idea how happy I am to hear you say that. I want us to put everything that happened behind us. I was a fool. I know that now. And it doesn't even matter about the... procedure. I never wanted children anyway, just as long as I can have you."

While Brian had been rambling on, Lauren had felt the color slowly drain from her face. If she thought she had been in a surreal dream before, she now wondered whether anything that had happened in her recent memory was real.

"What... what are you saying?"

Brian drew Lauren's stiff body back into his arms. "Lauren, sugar, I want us to get married."

"You're not serious!"

"You don't have to say anything yet," he reassured her quickly. "I wasn't intending to spring this on you so soon. It's just that... Oh, Lauren, it wasn't until your father sent you away that I realized how much I loved you. And your father and I... we talk about you a lot and he realized —"

"I don't want to discuss my father with you."

He held up a placating hand. "Okay, okay. We won't. I'm really sorry I brought all this up now. You're tired and this must have come as a bit of a shock —"

"That's an understatement," she said dryly, now fully recovered from Brian's alarming outburst.

For the first time since his cruel rejection, Lauren saw Brian with startling clarity. He was a quiet, unassuming man but with hidden depths that surfaced when he felt especially strongly about something.

The fact that he was willing to marry her when she

could not bear him a child stunned her, especially after his violent rejection. Could he really have made such an amazing turnaround? It didn't seem possible, yet this could quite conceivably be her one chance at marriage. How many men would be willing to marry a woman who couldn't have children? And Brian appeared to love her... No, it was too much to think about now. She was starting to feel overwrought with the emotional upheaval of everything that had happened that day.

"Brian, I... Can we please talk about this tomorrow?" She heard the thin strain of her own voice and felt the threat of tears in the back of her throat.

Brian squeezed her hand and backed toward the door.

"Say no more, sugar. I can see you're tired." He smiled gently. "I'll call you tomorrow. Not too early. You have a sleep in."

Lauren did sleep late the next morning. Considering she had drifted off just as the first pale fingers of dawn had seeped through the cracks in her bedroom curtains, that wasn't surprising.

Brian's amazing words had spun around and around in her head until she felt she knew the whole incredible evening off by heart.

When she had opened her mouth to plead for more time, Brian had covered her mouth with his. The kiss, filled with more passion and emotion than he had ever shown before, had startled her so much she hadn't even thought to push him away.

"You don't have to say anything now," he'd said gruffly. "I know all this has come as a surprise. But it's not a sudden decision on my part. Your father and I have discussed it. We won't talk any more now," he'd said hurriedly when she opened her mouth again to speak. "I'll call you in the morning."

And, to her chagrin, he had disappeared through the front door before she could utter one word of protest.

She groaned now as she looked at the bedside clock and realized she had slept the morning away.

A soft knock sounded at the door. "Lauren, are you awake? There's someone on the phone for you."

Lauren's heart sank. "Tell Brian I'm not ready to talk to him yet."

"It's not Brian," came her father's voice, muffled through the closed door. "It's a Rick Masters. Do you know him?"

Lauren burst from her bed in such a hurry, she almost tripped over the sheets that tangled around her ankles.

"Lauren?"

"Yes, yes. Tell him I'll be right there."

"Is this it, or not?"

Lauren swung her gaze back from the magnificent, pale salmon-pink, double-story house back to the cab driver tapping impatiently on the steering wheel.

She stared at the piece of paper on which she had written Rick's address. "Yes... yes, this seems to be right."

"That'll be fifteen dollars eighty, then."

She scrabbled around in her purse and extracted a twenty-dollar note, hardly noticing when the cabbie assumed she didn't want the change. Her attention was back on the house.

Rick lived *here*?

She climbed out of the cab, heaving out her overnight bag as she went. She eyed the huge house uncertainly. She took a deep breath. Well, she was here now, so there was no going back.

Unlatching the gate, she walked the short distance to the front door and pressed the bell before she could change her mind.

The door opened and suddenly Rick was there in front of her. Lauren's mouth dried, her heart skipped a beat before kicking back in at a furious pace. She opened her mouth to speak, but nothing came out.

He was bigger than she remembered. Bigger and more strikingly handsome. His hair was ruffled, there were dark smudges under his eyes and his arm was in a sling. But the imperfections only made him endearingly vulnerable and more appealing. Definitely more appealing.

Rampant anticipation skittered along her veins.

Rick seemed robbed of speech as well. He just stood there and Lauren felt her whole body burn as his eyes caressed every soft curve and answering need in her body. She furiously swept aside the yearning that had slipped under her guard. She had to get out of this potential minefield. Now.

She was still struggling to find the right words when he spoke. "Lauren. You came. Thank you." His husky voice revealed a mixture of surprise and relief.

Her heartbeat slowed, her shoulders relaxed. He needed her.

"Of course," she said lightly as she looked up at him.

Their eyes met and held. Lauren was struck with an overwhelming urge to kiss the tired lines from his face. She watched his eyes flicker down to her mouth. Her lips parted in response to the heat she saw there.

He took a step forward. "Lauren," he whispered.

A wave of panic washed over her. *No! This can't happen*. She stepped back and grabbed the overnight bag that had slipped from her fingers. She bustled past him and into the tiled foyer of the house.

She took a deep breath of the cool, air-conditioned interior. "So, what have you gone and done to yourself? I hope it's not too serious. I have to go back to work soon."

Rick frowned. "I realize it's a huge imposition..."

"Well, just as long as you do..."

"... But I didn't deliberately get myself injured," he finished shortly as he closed the front door with a quiet click.

Her heart contracted at the bewildered hurt in his voice. She blanked out the insidious curl of sympathy. "No, I suppose not."

Her words dropped like shards of ice into the silence.

"Your concern is touching," Rick said dryly.

Lauren blanched. "I didn't mean... You could have been seriously hurt. You could have been killed!"

Rick raised one eyebrow. "You almost sound as if you care. But it is only a dislocated shoulder."

She stepped back. "I do and I know," she said huffily. "I'd be concerned for anyone who was standing on a thirty foot retaining wall when it collapsed."

She stared at him and suddenly she couldn't help herself. She grinned.

He lifted one side of his mouth. "Naturally."

They stood, staring at each other for five full seconds before Rick took the overnight bag from her with his good arm. "Come upstairs and I'll show you to your room. Melanie's asleep but she's due for a bottle in half an hour."

"How have you managed since yesterday?" Lauren asked as she followed him up the stairs. She was still mortified at her rudeness, but she couldn't afford to feel any tender emotions when it came to Rick. He was just too tempting.

"Mrs. Bradford, my neighbor. And, before you ask, she and her husband are going on two weeks vacation to visit their daughter in New York. They postponed it by a day to help me as it was."

Lauren said nothing. She had asked for that.

They reached the top of the stairs and Rick led the way into a large, airy bedroom painted in the palest of apricot, offset by a darker border halfway up the wall. There was a huge wicker chair covered in over-stuffed cushions in the corner and a spectacular watercolor of velvety white arum lilies over the queen-size bed. Double louvered doors led out to a balcony.

"I'll leave you to unpack while I make us coffee. Once Melanie wakes, you won't have much chance to rest."

"Fine." Lauren breathed a sigh of relief when he left the room. She dropped onto the huge bed. It was covered with a plush duvet. She longed to curl up in its soft contours and wake up with this complicated mess behind her.

She stood up abruptly. She'd be a basket case if she didn't get control of herself.

Rick plucked two coffee mugs out of the cupboard and thumped them down on the bench in frustration. Why did he let Lauren affect him? More to the point, why was he setting himself up for further rejection?

He pressed his lips together. They were both pointless questions. Of course he knew why he had snatched at the chance to see her again. She was under his skin. She had invaded his thoughts and turned his rigid self-control to a warm and fuzzy desire. He wanted to hold her and protect her, give her everything her heart desired.

He swiped the wasted fantasies out of his mind and flicked the switch on the percolator. He spooned coffee into the top and watched the steaming liquid spurt into the pot, all the while cursing his stupidity. He should never have asked her for help. But then, when it came to Lauren, his brain didn't function as it should.

He walked to the kitchen door and called up the stairs, "Lauren! Coffee's ready."

Silence.

"Great," he muttered before leaving the kitchen to find her.

When he saw Melanie's open bedroom door, he frowned before quietly peeking inside. He tensed.

Lauren stood in the center of the room, nearly three feet away from the crib. He couldn't see her face but the torment of indecision emanating from her was tangible. His own body was almost as rigid, as he resisted an overwhelming urge to stride across the carpet and pull her into his arms.

He knew he should leave before she sensed his presence, but he remained frozen. The bundle in the crib, snug under the light cotton blanket, was asleep.

He watched as Lauren lifted her hand, held it rigid for interminable seconds, and then dropped it to her side.

He let his breath slide out as silently as possible; unaware until then that he had been holding it. His heart pounded in his chest. He wondered that she couldn't hear it.

Her tension was palpable.

The baby stirred. She snuffled, rubbed her tiny fist against her cheek, and then settled again.

Lauren jumped back as if stung, then seemed to gather herself. She took two steps forward and leaned against the crib. She reached out slowly and touched the baby's bunched fingers, stroking each one. Rick thought he heard her say something, but he couldn't be sure.

She brushed her cheek suddenly.

The baby shifted again, then opened her eyes wide and snatched Lauren's finger in her tiny fist. Lauren laughed, although it was a peculiar, choking laugh as if tears were lodged in her throat.

"What a sweet little thing you are," Lauren whispered. "I missed you." She straightened and turned.

She looked directly at Rick and he saw she had known he was there. "On the island you said you wanted to give me my heart's desire," she rasped. "Can you give me back my baby?"

Rick flinched at the pain and grief etched on her face. He was speechless for a long time. Too long, for she turned away and said, "No, not even you can perform miracles."

Melanie was gurgling now, kicking her blanket off and waving her arms in the air. Lauren started to walk away from the crib. "I think someone wants out," she rasped.

Rick resisted the temptation to draw Lauren into his arms and comfort her, but her tortured words nearly made him throw caution to the wind. He knew he risked ruining everything if he pushed too soon. Time enough later. He almost smiled to himself. Now that she was in his house, maybe there was a chance for them.

And maybe he was being a total fool.

"Are you leaving already?" he said, realizing with dread that she was still walking away from the crib.

Lauren stopped directly in front of him and looked at him. The pain he saw in her eyes was like a knife to his heart.

"I..." She swallowed, shook her head and glanced back to the crib.

"Lauren?"

She turned back to him again. "It's the baby. I don't know if I can stay. You don't understand. I tried to explain before... I don't know why I came." She shrugged helplessly.

Lauren's eyes darkened to a stormy sea green and Rick was hard-pressed to keep his hands from reaching up to stroke the pale velvet of her cheek. Her lips were quivering with emotion and he imagined himself quieting them with his own mouth.

He had just made up his mind to step away from temptation when Lauren whispered. "Will you hold me... please?"

Before his sensible brain even had a chance to advise caution, he swept her against his chest with one arm. She sighed into him and he almost groaned at the sheer pleasure of holding her slim body against his own.

He didn't dare move. He held his breath and soaked up the feeling of having her in his arms. After a little while, he felt a tickling against his neck. He laughed gruffly although it came out more as a groan. "Lauren, what are you doing?"

She relaxed further into his body, if that were possible and said, "Kissing you."

The little nibbles moved away from his collarbone and up to his jaw. He closed his eyes tight and willed a restraint on himself he was far from feeling. He couldn't prevent his hardness from pressing into her stomach.

"Lauren, are you sure you want to do this?"

She was still for several long, tortuous seconds before she sprang back. "Oh!"

"I think Melanie is getting impatient," he said quickly before she could say the words of rejection he couldn't bear to hear.

The confusion in her eyes cleared and she crossed the room with indecent haste. She lifted Melanie out, holding her away from her body, ignoring the child's delighted gurgles.

To his intense disappointment, the softness in her eyes of a few minutes ago had been replaced with a hard determination. She strode back to the doorway, where

Rick was still standing, and tucked Melanie into the crook of his good arm.

"I'll call Tricia, a friend of mine. I know she'll help until the agency can find someone," she said stiffly as she started to step away from him.

"Wait! Please."

"No. I'm sorry, I can't do this after all."

Rick moved in front of her as she tried to edge past him. "Lauren..."

"Get out of my way." She pushed against his chest, but even balancing a baby with one arm, Rick was too strong for her. Besides, her attempt to escape was half-hearted at best.

"Lauren, you can't run away forever." He paused then continued in a low voice. "Melanie needs you. I... need you. And I think you might need us. Just a little. Am I right?"

Lauren lifted her head at his soft words. She stared at the baby between them.

"Please... don't," she appealed.

He watched her face as a myriad of emotions warred with each other. The tip of her tongue slid over her bottom lip. Her eyes darkened. Her body swayed.

"Lauren... honey."

She lifted Melanie out of his arms. "All right. All right! I'll help you. On one condition. You have to promise you won't touch me again."

"I can promise," he said in a husky voice. "The question is, can you?"

Lauren's mouth dried. She tried to voice an off-hand reply, but no words would come. Only one insidious thought had any chance of coherency. She *did* want to touch him. Badly. She wanted to run her fingers lightly over the rough contours of his face and sift them through the soft waves of his hair.

"I'll have to answer that," Rick said, his voice seeming to come from a great distance.

Lauren blinked several times before registering the insistent ring of the telephone.

"Oh, the phone. Yes, yes," she whispered, still in a daze.

When she blinked again, he was gone.

Eight

IT took a full ten minutes after waving off Rick's sleek silver-gray BMW for Lauren's heart to stop skittering around her chest. She would be alone with Melanie all afternoon and the prospect excited her.

She tried to dampen the sudden ripple of elation coursing through her body. For six months, she had wondered whether she would ever be content in her life again, whether she would ever completely eradicate the anxiety that had plagued her since the emergency surgery that had robbed her of her dreams. If the way she felt now was any indication, she knew it was possible.

She smiled as she remembered the short phone call at her father's house with Rick that morning. When she'd heard the pleading urgency in his voice, she hadn't hesitated to offer her help. At that moment, she had totally forgotten her own problems and fears. Her only thought had been of Rick.

Three words had been her undoing. "I need you," he had said. Even if she had been hesitating, any doubt would have flown when he had uttered that soft, final word...

"Please?"

After a quick explanation to her father, she had scribbled Rick's address and phone number for him and hastily packed.

And now here she was, with a baby. It was a wonderful slice of unreality that she intended to make the most of.

Of course, she knew she would have to say good-bye to Melanie and Rick in a few days but, as she had learned of late, she had to snatch the moment while life was smiling on her. She didn't plan to waste a single second. She ignored the warning at the back of her mind. She could be setting herself up for further pain. She knew that, and it did make her a tiny bit scared, but the pleasure of being with Melanie again outweighed the fear.

She snuggled Melanie close against her hip and grinned like a Cheshire cat as she walked from room to room giving herself the grand tour. Rick hadn't had a chance to show her around properly. The phone call that had saved her from further embarrassment earlier had been from his office and he'd had to rush off.

The last room they checked out was Rick's study. Lauren peered through the doorway with interest. She took in the computer, fax machine, huge mahogany desk and a floor-to-ceiling, book-lined wall. She hastily closed the door. She felt a bit strange invading his private domain when he wasn't there and besides, Melanie was starting to get restless. The child had lost interest in the tour and was rubbing at her eyes and whimpering.

"Sorry, honey," Lauren laughed. "I guess it's about time for lunch." She reached into her jeans pocket for the hand-written instructions Rick had given her.

"Let's see. I need to heat up your bottle but, before that, you can have a can of strained vegetables."

She looked at Melanie who was now smacking playfully at Lauren's chin with the flat of her hand. "I think we can do better than that. As far as I'm concerned, canned food is for emergencies. If you were my baby you'd always have home cooked food." She kissed Melanie on the forehead.

She walked into the kitchen and opened the refrigerator. With Melanie still on her hip, she reached in for carrots, broccoli and cauliflower. "This is more like it." She smiled.

Unfortunately, Melanie took exception to being put on the floor while Lauren prepared the food. She immediately started crying, forcing Lauren to pick her up again and juggle the child at the same time as peeling and carefully cutting the vegetables.

"Thank heaven's for microwaves," muttered Lauren with a little less enthusiasm, after she finally dumped the handful of roughly cut vegetables into the microwave-proof bowl and punched in the numbers on the panel.

She swapped Melanie onto her other hip. "What would you like to do while that's cooking, sweetheart?"

When Melanie eyed her trustingly, Lauren smiled. "Right. A game of blocks sounds fun to me, too."

She walked into the living room where a bag of colored, plastic blocks were spilled out over the floor. But as soon as she put Melanie down, the child started crying again.

Lauren picked her up and the noise ceased. "Looks like blocks are out. What then?"

But Melanie wasn't listening. She was too busy chewing on her fist and grizzling. Lauren felt at a loss. "I guess it couldn't hurt to give you the milk first."

She trudged back into the kitchen, her arm now aching. As soon as she got the bottle out of the refrigerator she realized she'd have to wait for the vegetables to finish cooking before she could heat it up in the microwave.

Unfortunately Melanie, her patience apparently having run out, had other ideas. She twisted in Lauren's arms, crying and restless.

"Okay, okay, I get the message," Lauren said with exasperation.

She opened the microwave with one hand and nearly burnt herself on the steam, before she finally got the vegetable container out and replaced it with the bottle.

In her haste, she heated it for three minutes instead of the instructed two and had to run it under the cold-water faucet to cool it down again.

By this time, Melanie was screaming and Lauren was almost in tears herself.

When she finally got the teat into the baby's mouth and Melanie was sucking hungrily, Lauren's confidence had taken a battering. She sank into the armchair in the living room and exhaled with a grateful sigh.

Silence at last.

"Oh, well. I guess it's not quite as easy as I thought, but I'm sure I'll manage," Lauren asserted with rather more confidence than she was feeling.

Lauren had spent so much time over the last six months grieving for the loss of her ability to have a child that it had never occurred to her the reality of looking after a baby could be so complicated. But now that she was over the slight hiccup, she would be fine.

She was already realizing the plan to cook lunch for a hungry baby was just a little adventurous. She accepted the fact that opening a can of baby food was the most sensible thing to do next.

By the time Melanie had finished her bottle, her eyelids had drooped and she was almost asleep. Lauren was now in a dilemma as to whether she should wake Melanie for the rest of her lunch.

"I think I'll change your diaper first. I'm sure you'll be awake by then," she said, her confidence restored now that the child was happy again.

Changing the diaper wasn't as simple as it looked. Once the cold air hit Melanie's skin she came to life. She gurgled and kicked her legs in the air, making it almost impossible for Lauren to get the diaper on. But, after much hilarity and not a little frustration, the task was finally accomplished.

Lauren took Melanie back down to the kitchen and sat her in the highchair. "Here we go, sweetheart. Nice, yummy veggies."

As soon as the spoon of carrot and broccoli came near Melanie's mouth she expressed her thorough distaste. She screwed up her face and swiped at the spoon, sending it and the contents all over Lauren.

Still trying to see the funny side of the situation, but finding it a little difficult with an orange and green conglomerate plastered over her favorite pastel-pink blouse, Lauren gave lunch up as a bad joke and readied Melanie for her afternoon nap.

By this time, Melanie was wide-awake again and had no intention of following orders. As soon as her head hit the pillow, she bellowed her protest. Loudly.

Lauren tried to remember everything she had ever heard about bringing up children, which admittedly wasn't much, and attempted to resolutely ignore Melanie's cries. Easier said than done, of course, and Lauren's tolerance level for the pitiful wail of an upset baby was less than nil.

She lifted Melanie out of the crib, crooning to her and walking around the room. It wasn't long before Melanie drifted off.

Peace was short-lived.

The remaining hours while waiting for Rick's return were nothing less than a trial. Melanie cried on and off all afternoon. Bath-time was a disaster, with water all over the floor — and Melanie's dry clothes. The lunchtime bottle was the last one already made up and Lauren had to struggle with sterilizing more bottles, boiling water, mixing exact measurements of baby formula and then cooling a bottle again all with Melanie screaming in the background.

Lauren made a momentous effort to remain buoyant but by six o'clock, when Rick's car purred up the driveway, she was nearly in tears for the third time and hungry herself, having had no time to eat.

Rick whistled as he turned the corner into his street. Catching himself, he felt silly for a moment when he remembered his grandmother's aversion to any type of frivolity.

He had a sudden memory flash of himself as a small boy humming a tune that was a favorite of Eleanor's. He had been promptly told to shut up.

Brushing aside the unpleasant memory, he glanced at the bunch of flowers on the seat next to him and grinned. A thank-you for Lauren. The least he could do.

Juggling the flowers in the crook of his one good arm, Rick struggled to hold them while he reached up to put the key in the lock. He smiled at his own ineptitude as the key slipped and he had to try again, finding his mark this time. Before he could open the front door, though, it was wrenched open in his face.

"About time you got home!"

He blinked. Lauren was standing in the doorway, her face flushed, her hands threading through her hair.

"I gather you had a bad day?" he said calmly.

He watched as her eyes flashed with violent emotion. Her chest heaved and she tossed her hair over her shoulder. It bounced around her face like a wild cloud.

It was only when she snapped, "You bet your sweet tush, pal!" breaking the spell, that he realized his body had tightened in anticipation and yearning for this woman.

"Well, I'm home now. What can I do to help?"

"Don't you dare patronize me!"

"I don't mean to," he said quietly. "I brought you flowers."

Lauren's shoulders sagged. She tentatively took the offered blooms from him. "Thank you," she said without meeting his eyes. "I never said I was any good at looking after babies. I don't understand why you asked me anyway." Her lips trembled uncontrollably on the last words and she turned away, swiping at her brimming eyes.

Rick still wasn't sure exactly what was going on here but he could make a pretty good guess. "I asked you because you are the one person in the world I can trust implicitly."

He took a step toward her. His hand hovered above her shoulder but he didn't touch her. He had promised.

"I'm sorry I had to leave you this morning before you'd had a chance to settle in properly. But this business with the retaining wall collapsing has caused all sorts of problems. I've already got three of the residents threatening to sue."

"It's all right," Lauren said in a small muffled voice. "It's just that Melanie's been crying all d... day. I couldn't get her to s... sleep."

"You should have called me."

"I didn't want to bother you. Besides, you asked for my help. I should have been able to cope. I... I've always wanted to be a... a mother. Now I find out I'm no good at it after all."

"Oh, honey, don't say that. Please!"

His fingers tingled. Should he pull Lauren into his arms? Did he dare?

"Where is Mel now?" he asked instead.

"She's in there." She waved toward the living room.

Rick covered the short distance in long, rapid strides.

He had to put some space between himself and Lauren before he broke his promise and spoiled everything.

Melanie was lying on a baby blanket, on her stomach, chewing on the ear of a plastic toy. When she saw Rick, her face lit up with a brilliant smile.

Rick knelt down and picked her up awkwardly with one arm. She kicked her legs in the air.

His heart contracted. "And what have you been up to, young lady?" he growled with mock severity while giving her a loud kiss on the cheek.

Melanie giggled.

"Now she behaves herself," Lauren said grumpily from the doorway.

Rick turned to Lauren. Despite the petulant tone of her words, he could see the reluctant twitch at the corner of her mouth. "Have you been a naughty girl with Auntie Lauren, Mel?"

Melanie grinned again and reached for Lauren.

Lauren's face crumpled and she ran from the room. Rick heard the ominous sound of Lauren's bedroom door closing, none too quietly.

"Now you've done it, Mel."

The child stared at him innocently and Rick cuddled her tightly. "We'd better do something to cheer her up, don't you think?" he murmured into Melanie's ear.

Still carrying the baby on his hip, Rick knocked quietly on Lauren's bedroom door.

"Lauren?"

There was a pause before he heard a husky, "Yes."

"I'm going to get some takeout. I've got Melanie with me."

"Okay."

He hesitated. He was tempted to open the door but he

resisted the urge. "I was thinking of Chinese. Any preferences?"

"No."

He stood outside the door for another full minute before finally calling, "I'll be about a half hour."

When he got no reply he turned away with a heavy heart.

While he was waiting for his takeout order at the local Chinese restaurant, he impulsively ducked into the liquor store next door.

"I think we need to do some major cheering up, Mel. A bottle of Domaine Chandon champagne should do the trick."

Melanie jumped up and down on his hip, waving her arms and smacking her lips together.

He grinned at the child. "So glad you agree."

Lauren used the time while Rick was away to have a shower and bring herself under control. She felt embarrassed by her outburst, but still a little depressed about her failure to cope with Melanie.

All these months, she'd grieved the loss of her ability to have children. Now, when she had the opportunity to indulge her maternal instincts, she had fallen to pieces.

She dressed in scarlet pants and a bright multi-colored over-shirt in an attempt to cheer herself up. She was under control by the time Rick returned with Melanie in one arm and a paper bag of takeout food containers hooked over his wrist. The delicious aroma of spicy smells trailed behind him.

Lauren lifted Melanie out of Rick's arm as he stepped through the front door. She followed him into the kitchen where he dumped the bag of food onto the bench.

"Why don't you take a quick shower," she suggested.

"I'll fix up Melanie with something and serve up our food."

He gave her a warm smile. "Are you sure?"

She nodded.

"Okay, then. Can you help me get this sling off first?"

Balancing Melanie on her hip, she undid the knot at the base of his neck, taking care not to touch his tanned skin. She couldn't prevent the warm, male smell of him from tantalizing her nostrils. He turned to face her and she handed him the cotton sling.

"Thanks," he said softly.

"No problem," she replied, her mouth dry.

As she watched him leave the room and dash upstairs, Lauren's heart gave a peculiar little somersault. Happy Families. The expression leapt, unbidden, into her mind. A wave of desolation washed over her and she fought to eradicate the threatening depression.

"And I thought panic-attacks were the worst," she muttered.

She knew she was beyond the point of no return as far as her heart was concerned. Even if she left right now, it would be too late. Better to be philosophical about it and even enjoy it while it lasted. *You tried that once before and it didn't work*. She frowned and brushed aside the warning whisper.

She kissed Melanie on the forehead as she placed her into the high chair. "Whoever made up the expression 'Better to have loved and lost than never to have loved at all' should be shot on sight, hey, Mel?"

Just as Lauren was wondering whether to put the laden plates into the oven to keep warm, Rick poked his head around the doorway. "Back soon. I left something in the car."

"Fine."

Melanie was chewing happily on a fruit bar and Lauren was rummaging in the cutlery drawer for chopsticks when Rick returned holding a bottle of wine under his good arm and clutching two champagne flutes between the splayed fingers of his hand.

Lauren swallowed an exclamation of surprise. What was he playing at now?

"Do you want me to put the sling back on?"

Rick flexed his shoulder gingerly. "No, it should be fine. As long as I don't try lifting Melanie or doing somersaults on the bed, I think I can manage."

Lauren ignored his cheeky grin and took one of the proffered flutes. She watched while he prized the champagne cork out of the bottle with one hand. She continued to say nothing when the cork popped and he smoothly caught the overflowing bubbles with the other flute.

"What are we celebrating?" Lauren finally asked as she watched Rick fill her outstretched glass. The clear, gold liquid foamed up the flute before settling into a myriad of tiny bubbles.

"Do we need a reason?"

"No, I suppose not."

"Actually, I'd like to celebrate the fact that we're here together. Even if it's only for a short time, I know I'm going to enjoy having you here in my home."

Lauren didn't voice any of the hundred questions circling in her brain. She was startled at his sudden softening, but she shouldn't have been. When she thought of the hints she had picked up at different times, she knew that beneath his stuffiness was a heart of marshmallow.

Rick finished pouring the champagne into his own glass then lifted it to her in a mock salute. She tentatively touched her glass to his.

"To the three of us," he said softly.

Lauren said nothing. She blinked, but couldn't shift her eyes from his. To us, she echoed in her mind. For as long as it lasts.

He moved the glass to his lips and sipped the wine slowly, never wavering in the gaze that held her mesmerized. Melanie banged on the high chair and the spell was broken.

Lauren took a quick gulp of her champagne and said, "You'd better eat up or the food will go cold."

He smiled slowly but said nothing. He pulled out the nearest chair and sat down. He then picked up his chopsticks and started eating, wielding them with an expertise that Lauren envied. For some reason, her own fingers fumbled with the Chinese implements, although she'd never had trouble using them before.

Lauren stood in the doorway to Melanie's room, watching as Rick tucked the blankets around the baby and kissed her cheek. Tiny eyelids had gradually closed, but Lauren already knew better than to assume the child was asleep.

Rick slowly straightened and Lauren held her breath. Melanie's eyes opened slightly before closing again, properly this time.

Lauren expelled the breath she had been holding and smiled at Rick when he turned and looked at her. For the first time that evening, she noticed the lines of exhaustion on his tired face and felt a little guilty.

He crept away from the crib and Lauren stepped back from the door, allowing Rick to step through and close it with utmost care.

She followed him down the stairs and stifled a giggle when he suddenly slumped on the newel post at the bottom of the staircase, letting out a heartfelt groan.

"Now we start praying," he said.

Lauren went back into the kitchen, suddenly frantic for something to do, but she had already cleared away the remains of their dinner while Rick had changed Melanie and readied her for bed.

Rick came up close behind her and leaned over to pull open the fridge door. "At last we can finish off the champagne. I think we deserve it, don't you?"

Happy to pick up on his light mood, Lauren laughed and replied, "And three gold stars."

"Make that five," he said as he re-filled the champagne flutes that Lauren had rinsed and left to drain on the sink.

He led the way into the living room and sat down on the sofa. Lauren sank into one of the plush leather armchairs on the other side of the room. Rick made no comment on the deliberate attempt to distance herself.

"I think I underestimated how adept Cathy was at looking after Melanie," he said. "I could do with her help now... Oh, hell, I didn't mean how that sounded."

"It doesn't matter," she said quietly. "I have absolutely no experience with children and obviously Cathy does or the resort management wouldn't have allowed her to look after Melanie."

"As a matter of fact, she has a childcare degree and three younger siblings, but that was no excuse for my lack of tact."

"I don't mind. Really. I have no illusions about my ability with children, although I didn't think it would be quite that difficult. I don't have any brothers or sisters and the only babysitting I've ever done is for a neighbor. Her children were all school age at the time. I've never had to look after a baby. I know I should have told you."

"There was nothing to tell. It was unfair of me to leave

you alone with Melanie on your first day here. If it hadn't been for that idiot engineer who is now out of a job, none of this would have happened."

Rick reached over to refill Lauren's glass; she was surprised to realize it had been empty.

Anxious to change the subject, she tucked her feet under her, snuggled further down into the comfort of the chair and said, "How did you find my phone number, by the way?"

"The usual way. The phone book."

"But how did you know where I lived?"

"I didn't. You'd mentioned you lived on the north side of Miami. You were the tenth Fisher I tried."

"Oh."

"Your father sounded like a reasonable sort of guy. Not at all what I was expecting."

She smiled, happy with the turn in the conversation. "Oh, Rick, he's changed! I got such a surprise when I arrived home yesterday." She proceeded to tell him the details of the reception she'd received from her father, omitting Brian's untimely arrival and subsequent proposal.

"I'd only dropped in at home to pick up some of my things. I hadn't intended to stay. I was going to stay with Tricia."

"If you had, I wouldn't have found you again. Not so easily, anyway."

Lauren's heart slowed. "No. I suppose not."

"I have a lot to thank your father for."

His voice was like a caress; she swallowed her champagne in one gulp.

"I... I suppose."

He tipped the rest of the wine from the bottle into her glass.

"Trying to get me drunk?" she asked lightly.

He grinned. "Would it do me any good?"

"No!"

He laughed. "Then, no. My only motive is to get you to relax."

"Tell me about your family," she said quickly.

"Hey, now there's a subject."

"Oh, I'm sorry. I didn't mean to pry!"

"No hassle. I'm happy to tell you. You must be curious about the cryptic comments I made about my sister-slash-aunt."

"Well..."

"The truth is, both Kelsey and Janice are my aunts although I didn't find that out until I was sixteen. Up until then, I thought they were my sisters." He put down his empty wineglass and stood up.

Lauren followed his movements with her eyes. He walked over to the buffet table and poured himself a slug of what she assumed was whisky. He raised the bottle and lifted one eyebrow in question. She shook her head.

He put the bottle back on the buffet table then lifted the cut-crystal glass to his lips and took a healthy swallow. He folded his arms before continuing. "It wasn't until Madeleine, the woman I believed was my mother, died of breast cancer, that I found out the truth about my family. By then, Janice was already married to Carl, and Kelsey was away at college.

"After the funeral, I convinced them I'd be okay by myself for a few weeks while Kelsey finished the semester. Anyway, during that time, I took it upon myself to sort out Madeleine's papers. Amongst all the old bills and investment documents I found some diaries and photo albums I'd never seen before... You can guess the rest."

"Were they Madeleine's diaries?" Lauren asked softly.

"No. They were Eleanor's. My mother's." He was silent for such a long time, Lauren was sure he didn't intend to elaborate. She ached to ask him for more details, but she didn't want to open up old wounds.

Rick crossed the room again and sat back on the sofa. "Will you sit next to me?"

Lauren struggled to determine the best way to answer him.

"No strings attached," he said solemnly when she didn't immediately react.

Knowing instinctively that he needed her comfort right then, she left her own chair and settled down next to him. He immediately put his arm around her and she snuggled into his body. She sighed.

"Nice," she murmured.

Rick took another swallow of whisky then nursed the drink on his knee. "Eleanor wrote the diaries from 1963 until just before she died in 1969."

"How old was she?" Lauren asked softly.

He took a deep breath. "Twenty-one. Just. I was five years old."

Rick's voice sounded strange to her. It had gone all husky and rough. Lauren moved closer and hugged him. She thought about the little boy he would have been then.

"Do you remember her?"

He rested his head back on the sofa and closed his eyes. "Oh, yes, I remember her, all right. She was my beautiful, glamorous, older sister. She wasn't home very often, but when she was, she was dolled up and ready to go out again. Even now, I can smell the overpowering scent of her perfume. And she always wore a lot of make-up.

"I remember the way she would squeeze me tight before she went out and tell me to be a good boy. At that time, I didn't know where she went, but after reading the diaries, it became obvious she was an exotic dancer in a nightclub."

"I see."

"Yes, well, you can read between the lines on that one," he said bitterly. "No need to, though, it's all in her diary. It seems she went home with a different man every night."

Rick launched himself forward in the seat, forcing Lauren to sit up as well. "She didn't even know who my father was!" he ground out.

Tears gathered in Lauren's eyes and she squeezed his arm. "I'm sorry."

He ran his hand through his hair. "Yeah, I am too. Real sorry I never had a chance to tell her what I thought of her."

Lauren gasped. "Despite the lifestyle she chose, she was still your mother. And from what you've told me, she obviously loved you."

"Loved me enough to deny being my mother."

"Rick, think! It was the sixties. The shame of being an unmarried mother in those days would have been an incredible burden. She loved you enough to keep you. She could have put you up for adoption or even had an abortion."

Rick didn't reply, but he sank back into the sofa and drew Lauren back into his arms. He kissed her hair absently and she allowed the warmth of his body to seep into her bones.

She sighed, thinking again of the lost and lonely boy at five when Eleanor had died and then at sixteen, in a house by himself discovering the awful truth. She tried to imagine the betrayal he must have felt. Her own pain from Brian's rejection paled in comparison. Moisture gathered in her eyes and she squeezed them tight.

"She loved you, Rick. And I'm sure your grandmother loved you too, even if she didn't show it."

"Maybe."

They stayed snuggled together for a long time and Lauren must have drifted off to sleep, for the next thing she was conscious of was the warmth of Rick's lips brushing her own. She opened her mouth to him and allowed the heat of his mouth to mingle with hers.

She kept her eyes closed. Her limbs were languid and heavy. Blood moved sluggishly along her veins and her heart struggled to make the next beat. It felt as if time were slowing. She wanted it to stop altogether, if only she could hold this moment in the palm of her hand forever.

She felt his lips on hers. They were gentle. They nibbled, his tongue slid along her lips before slipping into her mouth.

"Lauren," he whispered. "My beautiful Lauren."

She had to strain to hear, but she could not mistake the way the heartfelt words were dragged from him.

"Oh, Rick."

He pulled her closer to him and gently lifted her legs around so that she was sitting on his knee, cradled in his arms like a baby. His lips left her mouth and trailed softly across her cheek, onto her closed eyes.

Indolent warmth spread through her body, penetrating her bones and stirring her blood. If she died right now she would be happy.

"Lauren, honey," he whispered. "I wish I could grant your heart's desire."

She smiled into his neck, finally opening her eyes; she

traced the dancing pulse with her fingertip. "There is something... I want."

"And what is that, sweetheart?" he asked very, very softly.

She swallowed and lifted her head enough to see into his eyes. She watched the coal-black of his pupils dilate. His eyelashes fluttered down and up again as if in slow motion. Everything slowed until the very universe held its breath in anticipation of her reply.

"You," she breathed finally. "I want you."

At first she thought he hadn't heard, but as the universe sighed and started up again, he lowered his mouth down to hers.

"You have me," he said against her lips before he kissed her.

Nine

FROM the moment Rick's lips touched her skin, a rush of hot need swept over Lauren, rocketing her from a languorous pool of warmth into a raging fire. Even as her blood surged and pounded out of control and her bones turned molten, her common sense screamed for her to stop.

She watched herself as if from a distance, unable to believe what she felt was reality, as Rick's every touch sent new flames licking along her veins. Her sighs of surrender, her whole body, seemed to belong to some other, wanton woman.

For the first time since that fateful night at the bar on St. John, the uncertainties were stripped away. Her confidence in herself was restored. It was different from her learned belief in herself and different from the courage she'd found to look after the baby. Now, her self-assurance was born of something deeper. An instinct. That, no matter what she chose to do next, it would be right.

She dismissed the what-if and the what-next. She wanted Rick. She was willing to accept whatever he chose to give, for however long it lasted. She would snatch this slice of happiness. And she would treasure it.

She traced the curve of his shoulder, continued across the hard pectoral muscles of his chest and lingered at the tight nub of his nipple. She smiled serenely when he sucked in his breath, and then sighed it out again, as her questing fingers delved into his springy chest hair. She glanced up at his face. His eyes were closed and she could see she held him in rapt anticipation of where her fingers would venture next. She hesitated.

"Don't stop now," he whispered in a soft sigh.

"You're still awake then?" she asked teasingly while searching his face for his hidden thoughts.

His eyes remained closed, but he grinned. "Do I look like I'm asleep?"

She automatically glanced down, and then squeezed her eyes shut, feeling a telling heat flood her cheeks. Her hand stilled.

When she opened her eyes again, he was looking at her. Gazing at her with an expression she hardly dared interpret. She felt the hot desire arcing from his eyes to hers. Her heart shifted in her chest as it recognized the mutual need in his. Her fingers curled on his chest.

"Come here," he growled.

Lauren needed no second bidding. An irresistible urgency propelled her forward. She couldn't have disobeyed, even if she'd wanted to. But she didn't want to...

She found herself in his arms, her face buried in his warm neck. She felt the steady throb of his pulse; automatically she touched the spot with the tip of her tongue.

She sighed, hardly aware of anything beyond the sensations coursing through her. She was vaguely aware of her clothes sliding from her body and her own fingers fumbling for the button on Rick's jeans. The zip slid with some difficulty over his hardness.

She gasped as her hand touched the hot evidence of his desire. She faltered and became aware of the heavy pounding of her own heart. There hardly seemed room in her chest as she felt it expand and thump in her throat. For one panicked second she thought it would surely prevent her from breathing.

"Rick..." she gasped. "I... don't... know..."

He swallowed her words with his mouth and she sighed again as the magic of his lips obliterated any hesitancy.

The next she was aware, the hard roughness of his legs slid against hers. His hot skin fired her desire and she clung to him all the tighter to savor the delicious sensation of his hard, strong length against her much smaller body.

"You're beautiful." She heard the rough timbre of his voice and thrilled at the genuine wonder there.

He dipped his head and scooped her nipple into his mouth. She arched her back and gasped as an arrow of pure ecstasy shot through her body to her core.

Rick surged up and suddenly he was inside her. She thought she would faint with the sheer pleasure of it. He felt nothing like Brian. Nothing!

"Oh, Lauren. I'm sorry!" he groaned into her hair. "I didn't mean... Oh, hell, I'm rushing you," he berated himself even as he moved inside her.

Lauren barely heard his heartfelt remorse. A riot of tumultuous sensation swamped her body.

"It doesn't matter. It's wonderful. It's... Oh!"

Without warning the building sensations gathered, teetered on the edge of a precipice then exploded into a million shards of pleasure. She gripped Rick's shoulders and heard his gasp of pain as she put pressure on his injured shoulder.

As she quickly relaxed her fingers, his mouth was on hers again as if to prevent her uttering the apology lingering on her lips.

He continued to move within her. She kept her eyes closed and continued to absorb the lingering echoes of her climax while riding with him on the building tide of his own release. His mouth clung to hers, his movement gathered momentum. Suddenly he tightened his hold on her, groaning deep in his throat. He slumped against her, and then rolled to the side, pulling her with him, settling her into a more comfortable position.

His mouth never left hers and she felt tears of joy sting her eyes as the kiss went on and on. She sank into his body while her own was taken over by a delicious lethargy, a feeling of absolute rightness. She had never, ever felt so happy. Nothing mattered except being in Rick's arms.

After a few minutes, Rick stirred. "We can't stay here all night," he whispered.

She giggled as his warm breath stirred her hair and tickled her ear. "I can."

He kissed her closed eyes and the tip of her nose. "We'll get cold... Besides, this sofa isn't long enough for me."

She opened her eyes and looked dreamily into his face. "It was plenty long enough a few minutes ago."

"Yes, but if we make love again here I'll have trouble explaining to my doctor how I re-injured my shoulder."

Lauren was suddenly overwhelmed with remorse. "Your shoulder! Did I hurt you? I did, didn't I?"

Rick flexed it gingerly and grimaced. "The pleasure was worth it," he drawled with a wolfish grin.

"Oh, you! I might have really hurt you. I totally forgot... I feel awful."

He chuckled. "Awful enough to make it up to me?"

She blushed. "I..." She lowered her eyes, still shy of him, despite the intimacies they had just shared.

Rick felt his heart swell, ready to burst from his body. He dared not examine too closely what he felt right at that moment. He knew he should feel like a heel for rushing her, then greedily taking her before she was emotionally ready. And, hell, it had been over too quickly. Already he could feel his body stirring and yearning for more.

The unlikely mixture of tenderness and lust he felt for this woman both confused and unnerved him. She was the most exquisite woman in the world. Delicate, yet resilient. A contradiction of insecurity and steely confidence.

He wanted to protect her and hold her forever. Right now, though, he wanted to make love to her again!

He eased himself up from the sofa, bringing her with him.

"Come on, up to bed. The next time we make love will be in comfort."

He watched her face and felt the protectiveness take over again as warm spots of color appeared on her cheeks. He halted an urge to touch her naked body again and bring it back to the same level of wanting his own body was fast approaching. In wonder of where the resistance to such sweet temptation had come from, he gently guided her from the room and upstairs. At his bedroom door, his good intentions fled.

Without giving her a choice, he nudged open the door and pulled her inside. With belated chivalry, he finally asked, "Will you sleep in my bed tonight?"

He cursed his voice. She would surely know of his uncertainty. She turned into his arms, his hands slid over her naked back, over her small bottom. She couldn't fail to feel his arousal pressing into her stomach.

She said nothing for several seconds and his breath caught, suspended in his body as he waited for the excuse.

"Okay," she said simply before turning and slipping underneath the quilt.

He didn't move immediately. Instead, he remained in the middle of the room, savoring the sight of her in his bed. Her face and the way her hair splayed across the pillow mesmerized him.

He watched her eyelids droop and close. An enigmatic

smile touched his mouth. He almost laughed to himself. Instead, he crossed to the bed and bent to kiss her mouth with a feather-light kiss, then slid under the covers next to her.

He gathered her close; she sighed and settled against him. He willed his body to behave when she relaxed into the beginnings of sleep.

"Rick," she murmured.

"Yes, my darling?" he whispered against her ear.

Her lips moved into a small smile. "You're definitely not boring in bed."

He pulled back in surprise. He opened his mouth to make an indignant reply and closed it again when he realized she had, indeed, fallen asleep.

His mouth turned up into a rueful smile. The woman had given him so much with her simple statement. Without him even being aware of it, Marion's cruel words had lost their sting. It seemed ridiculous he had ever let them affect him.

When Lauren woke, it was dark, the space in the bed next to her was still warm, but empty. For a few seconds, she felt disoriented, and then everything came flooding back. She stretched and smiled, enjoying the silky warmth of the sheets against her bare skin.

She eased herself up and glanced around the moonlit room. She stared at the digital clock, blinking several times before finally registering it was three am. She pushed her hair away from her face and frowned. Where was Rick? A trickle of apprehension traveled along her spine. Then she heard the muffled sound of a baby crying before it stopped again.

Climbing out of bed and carefully opening the door, she peered into the darkened hallway. Further along the corridor, the door to Melanie's room shed a sliver of light onto the thickly carpeted hall. Lauren crept across to the open door and pushed it further ajar. The soft light of the night-light gave the room a warm, ethereal glow.

Rick was sitting on a chair gently rocking Melanie's crib with one hand. He was leaning forward with his head resting in the palm of his other hand. His eyes were closed. A slow smile curved Lauren's mouth, as she stayed silent, enjoying the surreptitious peek at a totally unguarded Rick. He was wearing boxer shorts and nothing else. Lauren unconsciously tried to put moisture back in her mouth as she stared at the hard ripple of muscle on his back, the shadow of his strong jaw-line, the bunched strength of his thighs.

He opened his eyes and stopped rocking the crib. She held her breath as she watched and waited. He stayed that way for several minutes, his eyes never leaving the child.

When he slowly stood up, Lauren remained mesmerized. Muscles shifted and flexed with an economy of movement, Rick straightened and rolled his good shoulder, ironing out the kinks. When he finally turned to her, he stilled. He stared at her and she projected her desire in every line of her body. She sensed an answering need in him.

"You look like a gift from the angels," he whispered.

In that moment, she suddenly realized she was naked.

In her half-sleep state, she had stumbled from the darkened room, forgetting she had fallen asleep in his arms without a stitch on. She swallowed.

"I do seem to be at a disadvantage," she husked coyly, even while knowing a blush must have stained her cheeks.

"I'll have to remedy that."

Her eyes widened as he slid down his boxers, let them pool at his feet, then flicked them aside with his foot.

"Is this better?"

She could mutely nod.

He stood two feet from her in naked splendor, his desire fully potent and demanding. Her eyes flicked down and back to his face. Rick's own face was tense and unreadable.

"Rick?" she asked, uncertainty flooding her body, even as she felt a stirring heat gather within.

"Will you let me love you again?" he asked.

She opened her mouth and closed it again. Her head moved slowly down and up again.

In a flash, he bounded forward and scooped her up, hard against his body. She felt every nerve ending explode into life. The rough satin of his skin grazed and slid across her own and her mind overloaded with the task of absorbing all the sensations at once. Was it really only hours since they had made love? He kissed her hair, her eyes, then her mouth.

When he finally came up for air, she gasped, "Melanie..."

He chuckled softly. "You're right. We wouldn't want to disturb her!"

They crept back to Rick's room and tumbled back onto the bed. Before Lauren had even regained her equilibrium, Rick had pulled her into his arms.

This time, there was a sense of time being everlasting. The urgency of the evening before had dissipated and what followed was a mellow coming together of souls.

Lauren floated somewhere between pleasant reality and the edge of the dream-plane. She felt warm and loved and totally at ease.

Afterwards, she slipped back into a dreamless sleep snuggled into the crook of Rick's uninjured shoulder.

It felt like only minutes later, when Lauren heard Melanie's cries from the depths of a dreamless sleep. But in seconds, she was fully awake and out of bed. The clock showed eight am so she supposed she should be grateful Melanie had slept late.

She turned as Rick stirred. She dampened the flutter that moved in the region of her chest.

"Lauren?" he murmured, still half asleep. "Is that Melanie?"

She resisted the urge to slip back into bed next to him and ignored the strong lines of his back where the quilt had slipped during the night.

Instead, she picked up a white shirt hung carelessly over a chair and quickly slipped it on. "It's okay, I'll get her. It's what I'm here for, after all."

Before he could answer, she left the room, closing the door behind her with a quiet click.

When she opened the door to Melanie's room, the baby stopped crying. As soon as she saw Lauren she grinned and waved her arms with delight. Lauren's heart turned over.

She ignored the warnings clamoring to be heard in her mind as her heart swelled with love for the child... and the man asleep across the hall.

She picked up Melanie and quickly changed her diaper before taking her downstairs for breakfast.

Melanie had just finished her bottle and Lauren was reaching for coffee mugs when the front door bell rang. She glanced at the clock. It was still quite early and Lauren's heart fell as she imagined another emergency at work for Rick to attend to.

"Surely, they can leave him alone on a Sunday," she muttered as she headed to the front door. She re-adjusted Melanie on her hip and flicked a wayward wisp of hair out of her eyes. She opened the door and came face to face with the most stunning woman she had ever seen.

The woman, reed-thin and immaculately groomed, was smiling, but her face fell when she took in Lauren, dressed as she was, in nothing but Rick's shirt. Lauren licked her lips, suddenly aware of her attire, and unconsciously curled her hair over her ear.

She stared at a wisp of lace peeking out of the deep V of the woman's pale pink suit. She blinked at the perfect, white-blonde hair falling in a straight curtain over the woman's shoulders and the wide, baby blue eyes framed by impossibly long lashes.

By the time she flushed at her own rudeness, Lauren realized the woman was staring too, but with hard contempt.

"C... Can I help you?" Lauren finally blurted, rearranging her face into a polite mask. "Are you looking for Rick?"

She felt herself blush under the intense scrutiny. Instinctively, she knew the woman's arrival did not bode well for her.

The woman ignored the question. "And who, may I ask, are you?" she asked in imperious tones.

Lauren blinked. "Lauren Fisher. I'm a friend of Rick's."

The woman, having obviously decided Lauren rated as a non-entity, brushed past her and into the foyer. She hadn't looked at Melanie once.

Just then, Rick came down the stairs, buttoning his blue chambray shirt as he went.

"Lauren, who is... it?" His voice trailed off as he came to a halt in the middle of the cool tiles of the foyer.

"Marion," he said tonelessly as he tucked his shirt into his jeans. "To what do I owe the... pleasure?"

Marion's confidence appeared to slip at Rick's impassive tone. Lauren watched them carefully, trying to understand the strange vibes swarming in the air around them. She couldn't tell if it was barely restrained sexual tension or mere hostility. She looked again at Marion's suit and admired her fashion sense while marveling at the inappropriateness of the stiletto heels for a Sunday morning.

"I came to invite you out for breakfast, darling," the woman purred, but with less hauteur than she had so far displayed.

"I don't usually eat breakfast."

"You always did when we were together," she simpered.

Rick lifted one eyebrow. "A lot of things have changed since we were together."

"Of course they have. That's one of the things I wanted to talk to you about."

"My breakfast habits?" Rick replied dryly.

The brittle tinkling of Marion's laugh grated on Lauren's nerves. "No, silly. It's about my... situation. Things have changed..."

"Oh?"

Marion stared pointedly at Lauren, but there was no way Lauren would give the other woman the satisfaction of excusing herself. If Rick wanted privacy, it was up to him to say so.

"Let's just say... I think you'll be very interested to hear my news," she drawled with what Lauren assumed was a very practiced seduction routine.

"And just what is your news, Marion?" Rick sighed, seeming to suddenly lose interest in the conversation.

"Well..." She suddenly turned to Lauren. "Would you mind?"

Lauren, now that she had sensed Rick wasn't about to welcome his ex-fiancée with open arms, had regained some of her composure. A little imp of mischief made her smile innocently, "Would I mind what?"

Marion's jaw worked and Lauren sensed the difficulty the woman was having in hiding a naturally shrewish personality.

"If you don't mind, dear, I would like to talk to Rick alone," she said with saccharine sweetness. "Surely there's something in the kitchen you could be doing?"

Lauren opened her mouth to speak but Rick got in first. "Lauren is a guest in my home and I have no intention of relegating her to the kitchen like a servant. If you wish to speak to me, you are welcome to stay for coffee, but Lauren will be joining us."

"But —" Lauren began, prepared to be magnanimous now she was riding high on Rick's defense of her.

"My final word on the matter."

"Fine," said Marion lightly. "Whatever you say, pussycat."

Lauren's eyes widened and then widened again when she noticed the blush staining Rick's cheeks. She might have giggled, but now events were taking such an interesting turn, she had no intention of bringing attention to herself and giving Rick cause to guard his words.

"I'll get the coffee," she said smoothly.

Rick turned to her and she read the need to escape in his eyes. "No, I —"

"I wouldn't want you to injure your arm again... darling," Lauren interrupted cheekily.

Rick's eyes flickered dangerously before a reluctant smile twitched at his mouth.

"You'll keep," he muttered under his breath.

A buzz of awareness filled the air between them and Lauren was forced to look away, grabbing at the excuse of needing to put Melanie down on the floor in the living room to escape the sudden tension.

As she settled the child on a blanket with an assortment of colored toys, she watched Marion's slim, tanned legs cross the room out of the corner of her eyes. She stood and straightened and didn't miss the proprietary hand on Rick's jaw or the simpering undertone of its owner.

"I heard about the accident, darling, and I rushed over here to see what I could do to help."

Lauren had a sudden picture of Marion in her pale pink suit and manicured fingernails elbow-deep in baby food, dirty diapers and bath water. She choked back a hysterical giggle.

"Something wrong, Lauren?"

She spun around and faced Rick. "I was just thinking you could take Marion up on her offer and then you wouldn't need me," she said merrily.

Rick's eyes narrowed but his face remained bland. "I don't think that's the kind of help Marion had in mind."

"Oh, I don't know. I'm sure anything I can do, she can do b —"

"Coffee, wasn't it?" Rick's voice cut sharply across Lauren's provocative words.

She inwardly groaned. She had finally gotten under his skin, but had she gone too far? Marion's rudeness was no excuse for her own and she suddenly felt ashamed of taking her cue from the other woman.

"Coffee, coming right up," she said quickly.

She left the room but not before she heard Marion simper, "And whose baby is this, honey bunch?"

Lauren was out of the room before she heard Rick's reply.

Once she reached the kitchen, she exhaled loudly. She leaned against the sink and pressed her fingers against her hot cheeks. It was only then she realized how much tension had gathered in her body in the space of those few minutes.

As the seconds ticked by, she re-evaluated everything that had happened since the fateful ring of the doorbell. She pondered on the potential minefield of the situation.

Marion was here. Rick's ex-fiancée. The woman had hurt him but who knew better than her how hard it was to dismiss unwanted feelings for another person? For all Lauren knew, Rick may still be in love with Marion. Not only that, Marion had offered to help Rick in any way she could. And what better way to help than with Melanie?

Lauren's thoughts winged back to the night before, those beautiful, wonderful hours in Rick's bed. The intimacy, the special moments that went beyond sex. He would not betray those memories now. He would not dismiss the growing closeness between them. *He couldn't.* His relationship with Marion had been over months ago, she reassured herself. He had moved on with his life. He had moved on to Lauren.

She stopped her thoughts right there. Moved on. Those two words could take on so many different nuances of meaning. Not the least of which, that Lauren was a temporary diversion while he secretly still held a candle for Marion – the woman he had once intended to marry. And, what if Marion was, right now, simpering and eyelash batting in an effort to convince Rick their break-up was all a terrible mistake?

Lauren shot away from the sink. What was she doing daydreaming in the kitchen while that... vulture took away her dream? She dismissed the obstacles that prevented her own long-term relationship with Rick. She knew she was in heaven only temporarily, but she had no intention of having even that cut short.

She burst back into the living room and both Rick and Marion turned their heads in surprise. Lauren breathed a sigh of relief when she noted Marion was sitting on the sofa – alone, while Rick stood by the window with one hand bunched in his trouser pocket.

"I hope I'm not interrupting anything," Lauren breezed insincerely.

"You are!"

"No."

Lauren's head went from one to the other; she wasn't sure if she was relieved or unsettled by the tension in the air.

"How's the coffee coming along?" Rick asked smoothly.

"Coffee?"

"That is why you were in the kitchen," he reminded her.

Lauren shook herself back into the present. "Oh. The coffee. I'm afraid we're all out of coffee," she said as she planted herself on the sofa next to Marion – just to cover all bases, she told herself.

"We are?" Rick asked in confusion. "But – "

"And we're all out of tea as well."

Rick stared at her for two full seconds before he said to Marion, "Sorry about that. What with my sojourn on the island and the accident, I seem to have been somewhat remiss in the shopping department."

Lauren could sense the stiffening in Marion's body despite a wide expanse of leather sofa between them.

"No harm done," Marion said silkily. "Why don't I drive us to our favorite coffee shop? We can continue our... chat there."

"Will the baby seat fit in your car?" Lauren cut in sweetly.

Marion laughed with a brittleness that made Lauren want to grind her teeth.

"I wasn't exactly inviting the baby. Isn't it time for it to have a sleep or... whatever it is that babies do?"

"No," Lauren replied easily. "And we could hardly leave Melanie here alone."

"Perhaps you should just say what you came for, Marion," Rick interrupted.

"Do you really think it's appropriate for this... woman to hear our private conversation, darling?"

"I don't know. You tell me," Rick drawled sardonically.

Lauren watched Rick with fascination. She noted the almost imperceptible tightening of his jaw, the impatient flexing of his fingers. She hardly dared breathe, not wanting to miss a single nuance of the subtle by-play.

Marion hesitated for a moment; it was enough to show she wasn't as sure of her ground as Lauren had first thought.

"Well, she is just a baby-sitter,"

Rick seemed to give up restraining himself. "Lauren is more than a baby-sitter. She happens to be a friend."

Lauren felt a thrill of delight zing through her body. She marveled at how such a simple statement could take on, for her, so much meaning. After last night, the word "friend" should have offended her, but the warmth emanating from those simple words had been unmistakable.

Despite Rick's assertion that Lauren was to be included in their conversation, Marion apparently had second thoughts and decided to try another tack. Lauren was amazed to see Marion's face suddenly soften and smile.

"So, tell me, Sweetie, how have you been? Apart from the accident, I mean." Marion giggled prettily and Lauren had to consciously stop herself from scoffing aloud.

Rick's shoulders relaxed and he said, "Busy. Work keeps me on my toes. We're currently negotiating the purchase of another aged care facility. It's terribly run down. In fact, the living conditions of the residents are a disgrace. The minute the contract is signed next week, I'll be putting a total upgrade into motion."

"Will you need to go there?" asked Lauren.

His eyes alighted on her and his face relaxed. "Not right away. I've got some excellent people who will get everything organized."

Lauren returned his smile. "I think it's great, what you're doing for those people."

"Rick, I haven't told you what I've been up to," Marion interrupted. "I've got my eye on a new Mercedes Benz convertible and I wondered if you could check it out for me. Daddy says–"

Rick cleared his throat. "I'm sorry, Marion, but – "

Suddenly Marion screeched and jumped out of her seat. Lauren instinctively followed suit, expecting a huge, hairy spider, at least, to leap out of somewhere.

Before she could ask what on earth the matter was, she looked down at the floor where Marion's elegantly enclosed feet had been moments before and she burst out laughing.

While the adults had been engrossed in conversation, Melanie had evidently grown bored of her small patch of floor and had managed to roll herself over to the sofa. It seemed that Marion's bright pink shoes had been a source of fascination and Melanie had simply reached out and grabbed the woman's ankle.

Unfortunately, Marion's sudden leap from the sofa

with accompanying high-pitched screech had frightened Melanie just as much. She was now bellowing heartily.

Lauren quickly scooped up the child and pacified her against her chest, whispering soothing words and kissing her soft dark curls. She forgot about the by-play that had engrossed her moments before and concentrated only on the upset child.

After a minute or so, Melanie's sobs eased to a few hiccups and she settled against Lauren's shoulder. Registering the silence in the room, Lauren turned back to Rick.

He was standing in exactly the same spot but the expression on his face was something she had never seen before. It was totally unguarded and he was looking at her with something that Lauren didn't dare speculate on. Smoky warmth unfurled in the pit of her stomach. Her bones turned to thick honey and she felt herself blend in with the very air around them. They seemed to be wrapped in a cocoon, isolated from everything that was real. Time ceased to have meaning.

"I suggest you take your baby-sitting duties more seriously in future." Marion's harsh voice sliced through the bubble of sensuality. Lauren blinked. When she looked at Rick again, his eyes were shuttered.

She turned to Marion. "If you have a problem with children, you won't want to be visiting Rick again, will you?"

"Lauren!"

Lauren blushed. As soon as she had spat the venomous words at Marion, she'd known she'd gone too far. She didn't need Rick's reprimand to tell her that.

"Perhaps I'd better take you up on that invitation, after all, Marion," said Rick brusquely. "I'll just get my jacket."

Lauren swallowed. Sudden, unwanted tears sprang to her eyes. Another memory flash of Rick's soft eyes traveling over her body assailed her. Right now, those eyes may as well have belonged to another man in another lifetime. They were hard and uncompromising.

Lauren opened her mouth to speak. She wanted to apologize. She wanted to race from the room and cry. No words came out and her legs refused to function.

"That would be lovely, Rick," Marion purred.

As soon as Rick left the room, Lauren felt stranded. She couldn't in all conscience leave Marion to her own devices. A misplaced sense of politeness, perhaps to make up for her earlier bad manners, kept her rooted to the spot.

Marion crossed the room to the window and stared out for several seconds before turning suddenly with such a spiteful expression on her face that Lauren felt she had been struck a physical blow.

"I suppose you think you're very clever," the woman spat.

"No more than average," Lauren said calmly.

Marion's eyes narrowed. "You may be a novelty right now, but you can't seriously think you'll keep him interested."

Lauren smiled slowly. "Perhaps, but at least I don't find him boring in bed."

Marion flinched. "You bitch!"

Lauren mentally recoiled at the poison in the woman's voice but she guessed Marion was unsure of her ground if she felt the need to be so vindictive. It gave her further confidence to stand firm.

"I suggest you give up while you still have your pride intact, Marion. I love Rick and I respect him. From what I've seen so far, none of those finer feelings apply to you."

Marion laughed then, a brittle, knowing laugh that planted a seed of doubt amongst Lauren's newfound confidence.

"If you think that's what men look for in a woman, you're mad. The only thing a man wants from a woman, when it comes right down to it, is sex. And you, I hate to tell you, dear, fall a long way short of the mark."

Just then Rick walked back into the room giving no indication of whether he had heard their conversation.

Marion picked up her pink handbag and brushed a non-existent speck off Rick's collar. "My place would be a better choice for what I wanted to say, anyway." She whispered in his ear, but loudly enough for Lauren to hear.

Lauren turned and blinked rapidly. "I'll leave you to it, shall I?" she managed huskily before leaving the room with as much dignity as her crushed spirit would allow.

Rick watched her go with a heavy heart. He wanted to go to her, but he knew now wasn't the time.

"The coffee shop on the corner will do fine," he said bluntly to Marion. "What we have to say to each other won't take long."

He noticed the flicker in Marion's eyes at his words. He had been watching her carefully from the moment he had seen her plastic-perfect body standing in the foyer. He felt confident in reading her mind right at that moment.

The woman was jealous of Lauren! He'd had to stop himself from grinning a number of times in the last half-hour. He probably should have thrown her out the minute he'd clapped eyes on her, but the temptation of seeing how Lauren dealt with her had overridden common sense.

He was also ashamed to admit he'd hoped to make

Lauren a little jealous. Seeing how well it had worked made him regret the impulse. The last thing he wanted was to hurt Lauren. It was obvious now that he had.

He ushered Marion to the front door, tightening his lips at the liberty she was taking in clasping her elegant fingers around his elbow possessively. He glanced down and cringed. The dark pink of the long nails were the perfect contrast for her pale suit, but all he could think of was that they reminded him of talons. Sharp and dangerous, like her tongue.

He marveled now that he could see through her shallow façade so easily when, for the several years they had been engaged, he had seen nothing beyond what she had wanted him to see. Perhaps it was the simple honesty of Lauren that presented such a great contrast to Marion's canned bitterness.

At the front door he stopped and looked wistfully up the stairs. He could hear Lauren's voice interspersed with the soft giggles of the child. His instinct wanted to check whether Lauren really was all right. He imagined himself bounding up the stairs two at a time, scooping her into his arms and begging for forgiveness.

"Coming, darling?" purred Marion from beside him.

Rick straightened his face into a neutral expression. "Yes, Marion. I think we have some things to sort out once and for all."

Ten

LAUREN finished changing Melanie's diaper, keeping up a lively chatter until she heard the firm click of the front door. It was only then that she gave in to the utter desolation sweeping through her body.

What a fool she was to think she was able to handle such a short-term situation. Her heart had found its mate in Rick and would not be stilled. She had no choice but to admit the painful truth. She was totally and irrevocably in love with him. And, as for the child...

The enormity of Lauren's situation suddenly struck with an acuteness that threatened to overwhelm her. She sank onto the floor, clasping Melanie to her.

"Oh!" she groaned in despair. "I've been living in a futile dream."

She sat on the hard floor for long minutes, bone-weary, wrapped in a blanket of despair. She couldn't even cry. What was the point? Her eyes stung with unshed tears. What a fool she was. She had always known it had to end, so how had she allowed herself to feel so deeply?

Melanie yawned and rubbed her eyes. Lauren shook herself out of her reverie and kissed the top of the child's head. She sighed and tried to shed her melancholy.

"Time for bed, honey," she murmured against the baby's soft curls. She stood slowly and put Melanie gently into the crib.

"And time for me to get out of here while I still can," she added as she tucked in the blanket.

She bent and kissed the baby again then traced the warm bloom of the child's soft cheeks and the soft down of her tiny eyebrows. Taking a deep breath, she whispered firmly. "I can do this. I can do anything. I'll do it because it's the only way I can survive," she added with less emphasis.

She crept out of the room and swallowed the huge lump of tears lodged in her throat. She rallied her emotions and blanked out any doubt about what she had to do. What she must do.

Once dressed in jeans and midriff top, Lauren went back downstairs. She crossed to the telephone table and picked up the small, black address book sitting by the phone. She flicked through the pages. She didn't know Janice's surname but knew she and Carl lived in New York.

"The woman can just come and collect what's hers," she muttered as she flicked through the pages. "Then I'm gone from here."

In seconds, she had the address and phone number in front of her. Before she could change her mind, she picked up the phone and dialed. Her palms were damp as she gripped the telephone receiver, her heart thumped wildly in her chest.

While it was ringing, Lauren remembered Rick hadn't been able to contact them. That must mean they weren't home. For some inexplicable reason, she felt relieved. Just as she was about to hang up, however, the call was picked up and a soft, weary female voice said, "Hello, Janice Morrison speaking."

Lauren's voice froze before it even made it to her lips. Up until that moment, she had been operating on autopilot, now she didn't have a clue what she was going to say.

"Hello? Is anyone there?" came the soft voice again.

"Er, yes, I..."

"Hello? I can't hear you."

Lauren shut her eyes, took a deep breath and started again with more confidence. "Hello, Mrs. Morrison. You don't know me. My name is Lauren Fisher. I'm a friend of your... er... brother, Rick."

There was silence at the other end of the line.

"I'm staying with him at the moment."

"Oh, Richard, you mean. I see," said Janice.

"I'm looking after Melanie," Lauren said pointedly.

"I... see," said Janice again, more slowly.

"Look, I don't know if you do see, Mrs. Morrison," Lauren went on in a rush. "I suppose you don't realize, but Rick has had an accident."

There was a sudden, indrawn breath from the other end of the line.

"It's nothing serious," Lauren continued quickly. "He had a fall and hurt his shoulder slightly, but that's not the point. I understand you were supposed to pick up Melanie from St. John but were delayed. The reason for that is none of my business, but I think it's about time you came to collect her. We aren't talking about a puppy here. Melanie is only a baby and she deserves a settled home."

Lauren swallowed. It was all coming out wrong but there was no help for it now. "I guess all I'm saying, Mrs. Morrison, is that you really should let Rick know when you intend to come for Melanie. She's such a lovely child. If she was mine, I'd be on the next plane," she finished more gently.

To her horror, the woman burst into tears. Lauren gripped the phone and felt like the worst kind of heel as Janice sobbed and apologized incoherently.

"Mrs. Morrison – Janice — I'm really sorry. I didn't mean to upset you... Oh, I feel terrible!"

Janice's sobs finally tapered off to a few gasping

sniffles. "Please don't apologize. It's not you, dear. I've been worrying myself sick over Melanie, but I couldn't come and get her. I... I just couldn't!"

Lauren was silent as she sensed the other woman wanted to say more. Any resentment or lingering anger had evaporated. All she felt now was sympathy. She didn't yet know the details of Janice's dilemma, but she knew that only something of alarming proportions would prevent her from claiming the child.

"You're a friend of Richard's?" Janice asked huskily. "What did you say your name is?"

"L... Lauren, but —"

"He hasn't mentioned you before," she interrupted.

"We... er, met on St. John. After the accident, he asked for my help with Melanie."

"Really? That doesn't sound like Richard at all. He's normally very circumspect about who he lets into his life."

"He was desperate," Lauren said bluntly.

"Maybe. He didn't call me, though."

"I don't think he knew where you were."

"It's true, we have been away for a few days but we got back yesterday, there were no messages on our answering service, so it seems he didn't try."

A dozen questions swirled around Lauren's mind at that revelation, but she forced her mind back to Janice, who was still speaking.

"...problem with my teenage daughter, Kathleen. She ran away from home a week ago and Barry and I have been beside ourselves with worry."

"You don't have to explain. I'm really sorry I bothered you. I made a mistake. I'll help Rick with Melanie for as long as you need... for as long as he needs me."

"Lauren, you sound like a lovely girl and if Richard asked for your help, that's all I need to know. But I want to explain about my situation. It's the least you deserve."

Lauren's stomach gave a lurch. She had an unnerving feeling she wasn't going to like what she heard next. "Okay. I'll listen, but it's really none of my business."

"The police found Kathleen, yesterday. She was caught shoplifting. She'd been hitch-hiking."

"I'm sorry."

"That's not the worst of it. The reason she ran away from home is that she's pregnant."

Lauren felt her skin ice over and the hairs on the back of her neck stand on end. Her hand gripped the receiver and she had a sudden flash of herself in her father's living room six month before.

Unaware of the implications of the bombshell she had just dropped, Janice continued. "She's only sixteen, you see, and she was terrified to tell us. Apparently the boy has shot through."

"Surely you wouldn't have thrown her out," Lauren whispered through cold lips.

"No, no, of course not. Even Kathleen knew her father and I would stand by her. But that was the problem, apparently. I'm afraid I haven't coped well since Kelsey's death and my health hasn't been the best lately either. Kathleen knew I wasn't ready for the extra burden of Melanie so she imagined she could spare me by running away. Silly girl..." she added wistfully.

Lauren's head was spinning. What did all this mean? "What are you telling me? That you... you can't take Melanie?" Lauren didn't know whether she wanted the answer to be yes or no.

Janice sighed. "I don't know what I'm saying yet. Kathleen will be keeping her baby and we intend to give them all the support we can. I want the best for Melanie of course, but my own daughter has to come first. I know that may seem a little cold hearted – Melanie is still my niece – but I just need more time to decide what's best."

Lauren suddenly realized she had only been thinking of herself. "Look, don't worry about Melanie... or Rick. I can look after both of them until you're feeling better."

The tone of Janice's voice brightened. "That's so good of you. You don't know what a load that is off my mind. I've been trying to decide what to say to Richard."

"Just concentrate on yourself and your daughter. Melanie is in good hands until you work things out."

"Thank you again, Lauren. Tell Richard I'll call him in a day or two when I have more news."

They exchanged good-byes and Lauren slowly replaced the receiver on its cradle with shaking fingers, barely aware of doing so.

She was reeling from the incredible conversation. Twenty minutes ago, she had cast Janice in the role of indifferent monster and assumed she hadn't a shred of maternal feeling. Now she felt ashamed of her assumptions.

She had yet to decipher all the implications of Janice's situation. How did it affect her? What would happen if Janice decided she wouldn't take Melanie after all? Would Rick make other arrangements for Melanie?

Lauren pressed her fingers into her temples, willing away the beginning of a headache. It was all too much to take in. Right now, she had to decide what to tell Rick, if anything, about the conversation. Would he be angry with her for even ringing Janice?

While she tossed the many unanswerable questions around, she heard a car pull up outside the house. In that moment, she knew she had to tell Rick everything about her phone call with Janice. He was family and, besides, he would be angry if he later found out she had kept something so important from him. He would know it all, and more, in a few days anyway. She hoped fervently that Marion wasn't still with him.

Hearing the firm footsteps up the front steps, she rearranged her face into a welcoming smile and opened the door with a flourish.

"Ri— Brian!" she quickly amended as her face fell. "Brian, what are you doing here? How did you find me?"

"I didn't know you were hiding from me," he said, sounding a bit miffed. "I'm here to see the woman I love and, as to the second question, your father gave me this address." He peered inside the open door. "Very nice."

"Oh, yes. Yes, it is," she managed, now totally lost for words. She still had Janice's problems swirling around in her head and she found it hard to change gear to conduct polite conversation with Brian. Quite simply, it was the last thing she felt able to handle.

"Aren't you going to ask me in?" he asked, frowning at the bare skin at her waist.

She bristled, remembering his disapproval when she had first bought the cute top all those months ago. "Well, I don't know. Rick's not here at the moment."

"Surely he wouldn't mind you entertaining a friend in his home in broad daylight. I understand from your father you're doing this Rick fellow a huge favor."

"Of course he wouldn't mind," she said quickly, annoyed at the implied criticism of Rick. "It's just that... I've been up with the baby and I'm feeling rather tired."

"Ah, the baby."

"What about her?"

"I hope you're not getting too attached, that's all. Under the circumstances —"

"I'm well aware of my circumstances and I don't need you to remind me, thank you."

He was immediately all contrition. "I'm sorry. The last thing I want is to upset you."

"Why did you come then?" Lauren was quickly losing patience with him.

"I... I wondered if you'd given my proposal some thought?"

"Proposal? Oh, I'd forgotten..."

Brian's eyes narrowed. "Not a very flattering thought."

"I'm sorry, it's just that with Rick's accident and Melanie and everything and... I've just had a very upsetting phone call with Rick's sister." Her lips trembled. She had no idea why she had blurted that out except that she suddenly felt the burden of so many unhappy people on her shoulders, it all became too much.

Brian put his arm around her shoulder. "Oh, Lauren, don't cry. Just say you'll marry me and everything will be fine. This Rick fellow must have other friends who can help him out."

"Well now, isn't this a cozy little scene?"

Lauren sprang away from Brian and cursed her guilty reaction. She hastily wiped her eyes and looked up at Rick. "It's not what —"

"No need to explain. I'm not your keeper, but perhaps you should have picked a less public place than my front doorstep to conduct your little tryst."

"Now, listen here...," Brian blustered.

"The inimitable Brian, I assume?" Rick held out his hand. Brian had no option but to shake it, although he looked less than certain about Rick's motives.

"Yes, I'm Brian Butterfield. Lauren's fiancé."

"Brian!" Lauren quickly recovered her wits. "Brian, I haven't said yes."

He immediately looked apologetic. "I'm sorry, honey, just a bit of wishful thinking on my part." He grabbed her hand before she could stop him. "You must know we're right for each other," he said urgently.

"I don't know about you two, but I'm going inside." Rick sounded bored with the whole conversation. "Please yourself whether you continue this touching scene. Just as long as it's elsewhere."

Lauren snatched her hand out of Brian's sweating palm. "I'm coming inside too. Brian, would you like to stay for coffee?"

"We're all out of coffee!" snapped Rick.

Lauren suppressed a giggle. "Oh, yes. I forgot," she said with admirable blandness. She glanced over at Rick, then wished she hadn't when he winked at her. She went all warm and mushy as she felt herself drawn into a conspiratorial circle that excluded Brian.

She immediately felt guilty. She opened her mouth to speak but Rick got in first.

"Well, come in then." He opened the door wider and waited.

Lauren went inside, effectively giving Brian no choice but to follow.

Once they were in the living room, Rick said, "Sit down, Brian, my man. Lauren has told me so much about you."

"She... has?" Brian laughed with false heartiness. "All good, I hope?"

Rick patted him on the shoulder. "What else?" he asked with a chuckle.

Lauren watched Rick in amazement, wondering what he was up to.

"Can I offer you a drink?" Rick glanced at his watch. "Or is it too early for you?"

"A beer would be great, if you have it."

"Sure. Lauren, would you mind getting them from the kitchen? There's a darlin'."

Lauren bit back a sharp retort. What was he playing at

now? She was in no mood for games, especially when she had still to discuss her call with Janice. Cute repartee was the last thing she felt like engaging in.

She stalked into the kitchen, pulled open the fridge door and snatched up two cans of beer. "Relegated to servant status after all," she mumbled.

She returned to the living room and halted just outside the door when she heard her name.

"Have you known Lauren long?" she heard Rick ask.

"Years. We practically grew up together. Our families knew each other and we attended the same church. You know how it is."

"Sounds like you were childhood sweethearts," Rick said with such false urbanity that Lauren wanted to grind her teeth.

"Oh, definitely. I always knew we'd marry. Lauren took a bit longer to be convinced, but you know how women are. They need a man to point them in the right direction."

Lauren bit back an indignant retort. Rick must have heard her muffled explosion because he turned his head to where she was standing.

He ignored the thunderous expression on her face. "Here we are, just what the doctor ordered."

When she made no move to enter the room, he rose from his chair and crossed to stand close to her.

"Thanks," he murmured under his breath as his fingers closed over hers.

He spoke in that husky tone that stroked like velvet over her jangled nerves. The cold glass of the beer bottle against her palm was a strange contrast to the heat of Rick's hands.

"By the way," he added. "I love that little top you're wearing. It makes me want to slip my fingers inside and discover what's underneath."

His eyes held hers for long seconds. The warm brown of his irises darkened to a rich Belgian chocolate. She felt the tension in her body dissolve into thick, warm honey. The air became heavy with anticipation.

"Thanks for the beer," he said again.

She couldn't have answered if her life depended on it. She eventually relaxed her fingers from the tight grip around the beer cans when he gently tugged at them, but her eyes never left his.

"I'll go and check on Melanie," she managed even as a wave of raw need washed over her.

He nodded and she escaped upstairs with her heart crashing around in her chest.

Rick watched her go with a sinking heart. He wished he could have read her mind at that moment. Everything had been so right last night, now it was going off the rails.

His attempt at humor had fallen flat; he could feel Lauren slipping through his fingers.

"It'll take a bit of doing to tame that one." Brian's voice cut through Rick's reverie, jolting him back into the present.

Rick schooled his features into a bland expression and turned to hand Brian his beer. He twisted the top off his own and took a healthy slug before he trusted himself to speak. "Yep, I pity the man who attempts it."

Now that Lauren was out of earshot, he'd lost interest in making small talk with this pompous oaf. All he wanted was to herd the man out of his house as soon as politeness allowed.

"Oh, I think I understand Lauren well enough. As soon as she's my wife, I'm sure she'll settle down. She's been a bit flighty since... well, anyway, I'll soon sort her out."

"A bit of discipline, you think?" Rick commented with a deceptively mild tone.

"Never hurts to lay down a few ground rules."

Rick took another slug of his beer. "So, when's the wedding then?"

"As soon as can be arranged. Well, as soon as I convince Lauren it's the best thing for her. I mean, it's not as if she'll get many offers in the future —"

"Look who I found upstairs," Lauren suddenly said loudly from the doorway.

The two men swung their heads around in unison. Rick cursed the untimely interruption. He had a feeling Brian had been about to reveal something of monumental significance. What had he meant by Lauren not getting many offers? It was ludicrous. Unless... unless Brian knew something he didn't.

Brian had finished his beer and placed it on the side table before crossing the room. "So this is what's keeping my lovely lady from me. Cute kid," he added in an offhand way.

Rick watched Lauren's body language as the man neared her. Brian stared at the child as if it was an interesting specimen. Lauren tensed and tightened her hold on Melanie. Her eyes narrowed, her face took on a defensive expression.

"Yes. She is." She turned to Rick and smiled. "She hasn't been to sleep at all. She was just lying there talking to the mobile above her crib."

"Well, don't get too attached," Brian cut in. "And don't forget you have to give it back."

Her lips thinned. "I won't forget. And Melanie is a 'she' not an 'it'."

"Of course. Anyway, I have to be going. Walk me to the car?" He lowered his voice. "We need to talk."

Suddenly Lauren was very annoyed with his whole presence. He had invaded her space by coming here, her special space with Rick and Melanie, and she was feeling very out of sorts as a result.

"No, Brian. I'll call you when I'm ready to give you my answer. With everything that's happened, I haven't had a chance to give your proposal proper consideration."

"Okay then, I guess I'll have to be satisfied with that for now."

"Looks like it, old chap," Rick broke in. He placed a proprietorial hand on Lauren's shoulder and grinned to himself when Brian looked less than pleased.

"Lauren, we *will* talk."

She nodded. "Yes, Brian, but not now."

When the door was finally closed behind the other man, Lauren and Rick both sighed with relief.

"I'll just go and bath Melanie," Lauren said.

"In a minute. First, I think we should talk."

She stared down at Melanie. The child stared trustingly back. If only life could be as simple as it seemed through the eyes of a baby.

"Yes, we do," she said finally as she sat down on the sofa with Melanie. She clung to the child as if to protect herself from Rick's magnetic presence.

"Brian said something that intrigued me," Rick said slowly.

"Oh?" Lauren could feel her heart rate escalate.

"He seemed to think if he didn't marry you, no-one else would."

She swallowed with an effort. Her whole body tensed and waited. She wanted to run from the conversation but she was glued to the sofa. Melanie squirmed and she realized how tightly she had been holding the child.

"What a strange thing to say," she said in a strained voice. "Not very nice either."

Rick, who had remained standing, sat down beside

her. "That's what I thought," he said, watching her face carefully. "It didn't make sense. Do you know what he meant?"

"I... I've got no idea."

"Are you sure?"

"I spoke to Janice earlier," Lauren said in a rush, desperate to steer the conversation away from a topic she was not ready to cope with.

The ploy worked. "So, she called at last," Rick said.

"Not... exactly."

He raised his eyebrows.

"I called her. I found her number in your black book."

He looked at her as if trying to read her mind.

"I'm sorry, I didn't mean to pry."

"It doesn't matter. I'm just wondering why you called her."

"Well, you didn't seem to be concerned about her absence. I just thought someone should do something."

"I didn't know she was home and I knew she would contact me when she was ready. She begged me to give her some space last time I spoke to her."

Lauren immediately felt guilty, but rejected the feeling by reminding herself that Rick had failed to impart this piece of information to her.

"So, did she say when she was coming to collect Melanie?" Rick asked casually.

"No. She's not sure. She said she'll call you in a day or so."

"Is that all she said?"

"N... No."

He waited.

"She doesn't know if she'll take Melanie at all."

Rick was silent for a very long time. Lauren hardly dared breathe.

"What did you say?" he asked eventually, but very slowly.

"I... Kathleen's pregnant."

"What!"

Lauren stared at the thunderstruck expression on his face.

"But, she's only —"

"Sixteen," Lauren finished for him.

"She's hardly more than a child herself."

"I think that's where Janice's problem lies, Rick. She... she doesn't know if she can cope with Melanie on top of Kathleen and her problems."

"What has Barry got to say about all this?"

"She didn't mention her husband."

"I hope he's not out polishing his shotgun."

"That's not funny, Rick."

"It wasn't meant to be. What's the story with the father of the child?"

"Apparently he's not around."

"One less problem for Janice and Barry to worry about, I guess."

"That would depend on your point of view. I doubt whether Kathleen sees it that way."

Rick sighed and pushed his fingers through his hair. She could almost hear the cogs of his brain working overtime.

"What will you do if she doesn't take Melanie?"

"I don't know. I'll do what's best for Melanie."

"Would you keep her?" she asked tentatively.

He was thoughtful for a few minutes before he said, "She needs a family. Two parents. I can't give her that. I'm hardly at home as it is."

There were so many things she could say to that and she didn't dare voice any of them. She heard the anguish in his voice but she was at a loss to know what to say. She doubted she could have spoken anyway.

The baby wriggled on Lauren's lap. "I'm going to bath Melanie," she blurted out as she stood up. Even to her own ears, her voice sounded loaded with some strange emotion.

Rick came to her and touched her lightly on the cheek. "Wait. Talk, to me, please."

She struggled to get words past the knot in her throat. "I... can't."

"Do you want to go home?" he asked gently.

Her eyes filled with tears. "I don't know. I have to think about it." The tears threatened to spill.

"I hope you'll stay," he whispered. "I need you."

She shook her head. She stared down at Melanie, not daring to look at Rick.

"Okay. I'll stay. For now," she said even as she cursed her weakness. She knew it was madness but the strength of her desire to be with Rick and Melanie was too powerful to ignore.

Eleven

"YOU'RE not going to marry him!"

Lauren's coffee sloshed precariously close to the rim of her cup as she bristled at the arrogant confidence in Rick's voice. His face was an implacable mask and his autocratic attitude reminded her of that first night at Butterfly Bay when he had made her feel like a lower form of life.

"Really?" she said with heavy sarcasm. "And since when did I need your permission?" If he wanted an argument, he was going the right way about it. It was nearly midnight and she was in no mood for his high-handedness.

They had finally sent a fractious Melanie to sleep and all Lauren wanted now was to go to bed. Justifying herself to Rick was not on her agenda.

"You asked my opinion of Brian. Well, for what its worth, I think he's an insensitive boor. Surely you're not seriously thinking of marrying him?"

Lauren stared at the indignant expression on Rick's face. A moment ago, she had genuinely wanted his advice but how quickly she regretted the impulse. Perversely, she decided to ruffle his feathers further. "I might," she said with deliberate casualness. "I haven't decided. Brian could be just what I need."

He stared at her. "You can't be serious! He would stifle you and resent your independence, to say nothing of his insipid performance in your bed."

Lauren flushed. "He's not so bad."

"Your memory may be defective, but I remember clearly what you told me about him on the island."

"I do remember," she said huffily. "But he's not as selfish as he was. And... and he genuinely cares for me."

Rick placed his coffee cup on the table with a clunk and stood. He started pacing and she could sense the tightly coiled anger he was barely holding in check. Finally, he stopped and spun around to face her.

"You can't marry him!"

She stared at the raw emotion in his face. "W...Why?" she whispered.

He hesitated and she held her breath.

"Because he's not your type."

Her eyes widened at his clipped words. She folded her arms. "Oh, yes?" she said with deceptive mildness. "And who is my type?" The minute she voiced the words, she wished them back again, but she held her breath in anticipation of the answer.

"I don't know about 'who', but the last thing you need in a husband is a control freak. The man will never respect your right to be yourself."

She refused to show disappointment. Instead, she said, "What about you? If you're such an expert, why can't you see Marion is not your type either? The way she was all over you like a rash this morning was pathetic. You must have been blind if you couldn't see through her act. She's conceited and selfish and I doubt very much whether she likes children at all."

He appeared to consider her opinion. "You've only seen one side of her. As a matter of fact, Marion would suit me very well. I work long hours and often get invited to functions where a woman of Marion's style would be appreciated."

Lauren stood up and dumped her own coffee mug on the table. This time it did splash over the sides. "Fine! You're welcome to her. Why would I care if you want to be miserable for the rest of your life?" Her bottom lip trembled and she bit down on it.

"The same reason why I shouldn't care if you choose to spend the rest of your life with a Neanderthal!" Rick's voice was rising.

"Brian is not a Neanderthal!" A suppressed sob choked past her throat.

"Maybe not, but you deserve better."

"What? Someone like you, I suppose."

"Well, why not?" Rick snapped. "Give me one reason why we're not perfect for each other?"

Lauren fell silent. Rick's words lay heavily in the air between them. Neither spoke as the seconds ticked by.

Suddenly, Rick closed the space between them and picked up her hands, placing them against his chest. "We seem made for each other, in bed, at least." The corner of his mouth lifted in a wry smile.

She looked up into his eyes. Her heart contracted and the fight drained out of her. She blinked away tears that seemed to have sprung from nowhere. "There is that, I suppose," she said through the pain. Did he really think that was all there was between them?

He traced a warm fingertip along her cheek and she wondered whether an errant tear had slipped from her eyes. He touched his finger to his lips then placed it on hers.

"Come to bed, honey. We can talk about it in the morning," he whispered.

Something inside Lauren snapped and she shook herself out of his arms. "Don't you dare brush me off with sex! Just because you're great in bed, doesn't mean you can bribe me with it."

He looked surprised for a moment, but then he grinned. "Why not, if it works?"

He pulled her back into his arms and covered her mouth with his before she realized what was happening. The kiss was hard and punishing, although, whether he was punishing himself or her, she couldn't tell.

He dragged his mouth away from hers. They were both breathing heavily as they stared at each other in shock.

"I'm sorry," he said as he stroked her hair away from her face. "That was unforgivable."

"It's... it's okay."

He put her away from him and ran his hand through his hair. "Oh, hell," he muttered.

She put her hand on his arm. "It really is okay," she whispered. "More than okay," she added huskily.

He lifted his head and they stared into each other's eyes. She suddenly felt hot in the knit sweater she had changed into earlier in the evening.

She tried a tentative smile. "I..." She swallowed. "I think I can hear Melanie."

Before he could reply she ran from the room and up the stairs. Of course, she hadn't heard the baby cry, but she had latched on to any excuse to escape the heavy tension.

When she reached Melanie's bedroom she peeked inside to make sure the child was in fact asleep. She closed the door again and leaned against the door jam. She squeezed her eyes tight in an effort to fight the inescapable truth. When she straightened and turned, Rick was standing at his bedroom door waiting for her.

No words were needed. Perhaps if he'd asked, she would have said no. As it was, she walked slowly toward him.

When she reached him, he straightened. "It's not just sex," he said quietly. "It's never been just sex."

She swallowed. She felt self-conscious and extremely nervous, which was ridiculous at this late stage, but she couldn't help it. He must have sensed her uncertainty, for he captured her mouth with his in one swift movement. With his lips glued to hers, he backed into the room, kicking the door shut with his foot.

She felt his hands on her back. They burned through the fabric, pressing her against his body.

His mouth never left hers. It moved gently, yet with a strength of purpose that stamped his possession on her. His tongue danced with hers. She groaned and he pulled her tighter. They seemed to blend into one entity as Lauren lost her sense of aloneness to become part of her beloved.

When he released her for a moment, she whimpered the loss. She reached for him but he shook his head.

"Not yet," he said in a rich, gravelly voice. "I want to see you. All of you. Will you undress for me?"

A blush stained her cheeks. "I... don't know."

He smiled reassuringly. "Undo your buttons. Start at the top."

She wanted to say no. She also wanted to obey him. She thought about asking him to close the curtains. But she said nothing. Instead, she slid the first button open.

His eyes glittered. "And now, the next one."

She swallowed and released the next button and the next, until she reached the top of her jeans.

"Open your shirt. I want to see all of you."

She touched the edges of her shirt and, very slowly, she pulled them apart, exposing her lace-covered breasts to his blazing eyes. She watched his throat work. She entranced him, and it made her bolder.

She opened her shirt wider, pulling it free from her jeans, so that it hung open and her stomach and the smooth rise of her creamy skin, was bare to his hot scrutiny.

"Do you want to touch?" she whispered, feeling daring now.

His gaze lifted to her face. His eyes were glazed with desire. She felt the thrill of feminine power and it gave her confidence.

"Soon," he replied with a husky growl. "Take your shirt off."

She slid it from her shoulders and reached for the button on her jeans. She suddenly wanted to be totally naked for him. She wanted to slide her body against his.

He shook his head. "No, take your bra off."

She reached behind, and released the catch, all the while holding his eyes to hers. When the tiny garment fell to the floor, she heard his sudden, harsh, indrawn breath. She felt her own breathing increase and her heart rate escalate. The tips of her breasts hardened and she unconsciously thrust them forward to his hot gaze.

Somehow the fact that she was still dressed in her jeans and shoes made the situation all the more decadent. He was still fully dressed, but she could see the hard evidence of his desire begging for release. She swallowed and tried to moisten her dry mouth.

"Can I undress you?" she said in a voice unrecognizable as her own.

He smiled. "Not yet, my beautiful angel. Not until I think you're ready."

I'm ready now, she wanted to scream.

"Undo your jeans."

She undid the button and slowly slid down the zip. The breath was suspended in her throat as she watched his eyes follow her movements. She deliberately opened her jeans just wide enough so that he could see the white lace of her panties peeking through.

"Do you want to touch yet?" she asked cheekily.

He didn't answer for several, tension filled seconds. "Take off your shoes."

She sat on the edge of the bed and quickly took them, and her socks, off. She felt his eyes on her back as she bent over her task, gasping when the tight tips of her breasts grazed the rough denim of her jeans.

When she stood again, he was directly before her, except, this time, he was naked too. He stood there in magnificent splendor and she had no choice but to take the one step forward that would put her back into his embrace.

His strong arms covered her back and she had only to lift her face to his to again experience the exquisite pleasure of his kisses.

While they drank of each other, his hands glided over her back and smoothed her jeans over her bottom. She helped him slide her jeans lower, taking her lace underwear with them.

She sighed in delight when, at last, she was naked against his body. They stood like that for several minutes and she soaked up the sheer pleasure of being held against him.

In the next second, before she knew what was happening, they were on his bed, under the covers. The slow sensual waltz had ended, replaced by a mad tango of desire.

His hand slid between her legs and she opened up so he could reach her moist heat. His touch was gentle and she writhed as a burning need swept through her body. She clutched his buttocks and he groaned as her hands glided over his roughness.

When his fingers sought and found her hot core she gasped and clung tighter. "You like that," he murmured against her ear.

"Oh, Ye...es!"

She gasped on the word as his stroke increased its pace. Her head swung from side to side against his pillow. She was taken away on a tide of blossoming heat. She couldn't have stopped if she'd wanted to. But she didn't want to...

He kissed her tenderly, even as his fingers worked their erotic magic. The tension in her body built in time with the pleasure. When she thought she couldn't get another breath into her body, the pleasure exploded and she shattered into a million fragments before they coalesced back into her body.

As she caught her breath and dissolved into the bed, he slid over her and inside her. She gasped as the pleasure started all over again. Except this time it was different. Softer, sweeter somehow.

Her body moved in time with his and, when it gained momentum, he clasped her tight and buried his face in her hair with a heartfelt groan. She smiled with joy into his neck and held him with equal strength. She never wanted this moment to end. She never wanted to let him go.

She thought nothing of what may come next. She soaked up the beauty and wonder of the moment until she dozed in his arms.

It was almost a week later, on Friday evening, when Rick arrived home very late, just after Lauren had settled Melanie for the night.

She had received a call from him during the afternoon, so she wasn't concerned, but it had been a long day without him. In fact, it had been a long week where he'd hardly been home. The days spent with Melanie were bittersweet and the nights in Rick's bed surpassed anything she had ever dared wish for. But every day, as she became more entrenched into life with Rick and Melanie, she wondered how she would cope when it all ended.

Rick had spoken to Janice or Barry on three occasions, distracted and thoughtful after each call. He had only said Janice was feeling better and coming to terms with things. He hadn't elaborated and Lauren hadn't dared ask for details. If she was honest with herself, she could admit that she didn't want to know too much detail. She didn't want to know how soon her idyllic lifestyle would end.

As soon as Lauren heard Rick's car in the drive, she quickly changed out of her tee shirt and jeans into a light, summery dress of warm golds and pale greens that swirled around her calves. She dragged a brush through her thick curls, sprayed herself with a light perfume and skipped down the stairs just as Rick opened the front door. He was holding a huge bunch of red roses. Intermingled with the tight buds were sprigs of fern and baby's breath. A heady perfume filled the foyer.

"Rick! They're gorgeous."

Rick dropped his briefcase, nudged the front door shut and held out the flowers to her. "Nothing but the best for a lovely lady." He kissed her softly on the lips. "My lovely lady," he added huskily.

Lauren blinked away the moistness in her eyes. "Thank you."

"But there's more," he chuckled. "I'm taking you out to dinner."

"What about Melanie?" she asked, as she inhaled deeply of the heady scent of the roses.

"All taken care of. Noelle, the daughter of my new receptionist, will be here any minute to baby-sit for us."

She was speechless. "I don't know what to say," she managed eventually.

"You don't have to say anything. I'll put these flowers in water while you get ready."

"I... I didn't bring anything fancy to wear."

He smoothed her hair over her ear. "What you're wearing is fine. You could be in sackcloth for all I'd care. You're always a princess to me."

She swallowed the lump in her throat and ran up the stairs. She didn't trust her voice.

She slipped into high-heels and a jacket and bundled her hair high on her head in a loose chignon. With a small amount of make-up and another spray of perfume, she was ready.

She quickly checked on Melanie. Finding her in a deep sleep, she hurried back downstairs.

Rick was still in the foyer chatting to a girl who looked to be around seventeen or eighteen.

"Lauren," he said warmly. "This is Noelle. I've just been telling her where everything is."

Lauren found it hard to shift her eyes from Rick's handsome face, but she forced herself to smile at the girl. "Hi Noelle, nice to meet you. Melanie is asleep, she shouldn't wake again tonight."

"I've given her my cell number in case of any problems," Rick smiled before ushering Lauren out into the balmy night air.

To Lauren's heightened awareness, Rick seemed especially loving that evening. He took her to a small Italian restaurant where they were shown to an intimate table in the corner, out of earshot of other diners.

During dinner, he was attentive and seemed to hang on her every word as she told him of her day with Melanie.

Finally, when they had finished their cassata and were sipping cappuccino, Rick reached into his pocket, withdrew a small jeweler's box and placed it on the table.

Lauren's heart slipped into overdrive and her stomach turned over.

Rick picked up Lauren's hand. "Lauren... honey, I think you must know how I feel about you by now."

She licked her dry lips. "I... think so," she whispered, mesmerized by the warmth of his eyes.

"I love you. And I'm hoping you love me too."

She was speechless. Not in her wildest dreams had she dared hope for such a declaration.

"Do you love me, too?" he asked with a rueful smile when she didn't say anything. "Even just a little bit?"

Lauren squeezed his hand and returned his smile. "Oh, Rick, I love you more than you could ever imagine."

He grinned, his shoulders visibly relaxing.

She looked into his eyes. "How could you ever doubt it?"

He lifted her hand, bringing her fingers to his mouth, kissing each one in turn. "You don't know how much it means to hear you say that."

His eyes were suspiciously moist when he released her hand and reached for the small box still sitting next to his coffee cup.

With a horrible lurch of her stomach, Lauren suddenly realized what was coming next.

She felt the blood drain from her face. She grabbed Rick's hand before he could open the box. "Rick! There's something I have to tell you."

"What is it?"

How to tell him? How could she smash her dream to pieces? But she had to. She had no choice. Leaving it for another day or week or month would make it that much harder.

"It's about my miscarriage."

Rick visibly relaxed. "Lauren, honey, I understand. We won't start our family until you're ready. I'll wait as long as you want. But I warn you, I'll want at least six." He chuckled.

Lauren felt her face go even whiter. She felt sick. "There won't be any children," she said bluntly.

He went very still. "What?"

"I said —"

"I heard what you said. I just didn't believe it. I've seen you with Melanie. You love children."

Lauren's eyes filled with tears. "Of course I love children. But I can't have any."

"If it's the post-traumatic stress, don't worry. There's no hurry. I can wait until you're ready."

Tears were pouring down her face now. "Will you listen to me! The miscarriage was as a result of an ectopic pregnancy. I had a hysterectomy!"

Rick visibly recoiled. "What!" he gasped. His face drained of color. "Surely that wasn't necessary," he added weakly.

"Not usually. But there were complications."

The tears dried on Lauren's face and everything took on a sense of unreality. With a kind of macabre detachment she watched a number of expressions cross Rick's face, ranging from disgust to shock. She wanted to laugh hysterically at the cruel trick life had played on her, but then she had known it had to end sometime. She just hadn't planned on such a dramatic exit.

When he remained silent for several minutes, Lauren finally noticed that they were the subject of surreptitious interest by the other diners.

"I want to go home," she said bluntly when Rick still hadn't said anything after several fraught minutes.

Seeing her stricken look, Rick stood from his seat. "Of course. Of course. Oh, hell. I'm sorry, Lauren."

"So am I," she whispered at the floor. It was a lovely dream while it lasted, she thought miserably. "Can we please go home?"

The people at the next table were openly watching them now and she could see the waiter over the other side of the room eyeing them nervously.

"Yes. I'm sorry," he said again.

He looked so dazed; she could almost feel sorry for him. She actually wanted to comfort him! What warped imp in her brain had created that thought?

He didn't speak on the way home and she was grateful. She longed to get back to her bed – her bed at her father's house – and sob into the pillow. She didn't know how she would have coped if Rick had asked her further questions right then.

If he apologized again, she would commit murder.

Noelle greeted them as they walked in the front door. "You two are home early," she yawned as she rose from the sofa stretching.

"Any problems?" asked Rick.

"I didn't hear a peep out of Melanie. I checked her a couple of times, but she was fast asleep."

"Good, good. I'll take you home now."

"Great." She turned to pick up her bag. "Oh, I nearly forgot. A Janice called. She said to tell you, she's flying in tomorrow morning. Her flight comes in at nine thirty-five."

Lauren received this information with mixed feelings but she realized it didn't matter anyway. Rick's shoulder was fully healed and it would be easy to arrange childcare during the day while he was at work. The fact that Janice had finally got her act together was neither here nor there. It was time for Lauren to go home.

"Right." Rick's face was impassive.

Lauren didn't even try to guess at his feelings. But he probably felt the same. It was only fitting that Janice should finally arrive just when their own situation had come to a head.

"I'll be back in half an hour," Rick said to Lauren. She tried not to cringe at the cool politeness in his voice. He must be finding this as hard as she was. It would be better for both of them if she left right now, she realized.

When Rick walked back in the door after returning from taking Noelle home, he came to a sudden halt. Lauren was standing in the middle of the foyer with her luggage at her feet.

He didn't say anything for several long seconds. "Lauren?"

She swallowed a ball of tears that threatened to swell up and engulf her. "I'm going. My cab will be here in a minute."

His face appeared ashen but it could have been a trick of the subdued light. "Can't you wait until the morning?"

"No. I'm going now."

"But..."

"I think we've said all we need to say to each other. I understand your feelings completely."

"I doubt that," he suddenly ground out harshly. "You didn't give me a chance to explain how I feel."

"Well, I don't want to talk about it anyway. There's nothing to say," she said wildly with a note of hysteria in her voice.

He held up his hands placatingly. "I'm sorry. I don't want to upset you." He ran his hands through his hair. "This has been quite a night, one way or another," he mumbled.

"You don't say," she said sarcastically.

He stared at her with a hard look on his face. "You aren't being fair to me."

"Fair!" she nearly shrieked. She pressed her palm against her stomach. "Do you think this is fair?"

"No, but —"

"Don't you dare start on the patronizing platitudes. I've heard them all before."

"I had no intention of it. You feel sorry enough for yourself without me joining in."

"I do not! I'm over it. You're the one with the problem."

"If you're over it, why can't we talk about it? Why are you dismissing me out of hand?"

"There's nothing to talk about. You can't change the facts."

"No, but it's not the end of the world. We could still have each other."

"You say that now. How will it be in five, ten years time? You said yourself, you want six kids."

"It was a figure of speech," he said quietly.

"No it wasn't! I saw the look on your face when I told you I couldn't have your children."

"It was a shock. It was you I felt sorry for – not me."

"I know what I saw."

"So, you're judge, jury and a mind reader now?"

"It doesn't take a mind reader to figure out what you were thinking."

"And what about you? You haven't been exactly honest. You must have known I was falling in love with you. All this time you kept this to yourself."

"Yes, well, I do feel ashamed about that, but you can't blame me for wanting some happiness for a little while."

His eyes softened. "You were happy, weren't you?" he said quietly now.

"Yes, I was happy. But it was all a dream. An illusion," she choked.

He took a step forward. "It needn't be. We could still—"

She backed away. "No!"

Tears were streaming down her face and she could barely make out his stricken features through the blur of them.

The horn of the cab sounded into the silence.

"My cab's here," she croaked.

"I'll send him away."

"No."

"At least let me drive you to your father's house."

"No. Please, no. It's better this way," she sobbed.

He sighed in exasperation. "Okay. I'll let you go. But it's not the end."

"Yes, it is," she said fiercely. "I... I don't love you, Rick."

He looked as if she had slapped him, but she refused to take back the words. It was for his own good. Nothing could come of it. Nothing except pain and heartache.

"I don't believe you," he said through tight lips. He didn't sound convinced.

"Believe it. It was good while it lasted, but it's over."

She snatched up her bags and wrenched the front door open.

Rick watched her run down the path while the cab driver got out to help her with her bags. He stared at the empty street long after the cab had pulled away from the curb. His heart sat like a shriveled cold lump in his chest.

He rubbed his eyes and his fingers came away wet.

"Lauren," he whispered. "I can't believe you don't love me. I refuse to accept it."

He finally turned and went back inside, automatically shutting and locking the door. He walked slowly up to his bedroom and undressed, still full of disbelief that something so wonderful could have gone so wrong.

He knew he had handled her revelation badly, but it had been such a shock. If only she had given him a chance to explain that his anguish was for her, not for him. Sure, he loved kids, but if he had to choose between having children and his beloved Lauren, there was no choice. How to make her believe that?

But what if she was telling the truth? What if her feelings weren't as strong as his? What if she didn't love him?

The pain of that thought was too much. He couldn't doubt her love, for if he did, then he really did have nothing.

Melanie was going to Janice. He couldn't lose Lauren as well. They would work something out. They had to. His life depended on it.

Twelve

IT was a very subdued Rick who picked up Janice and Barry at the airport the next morning. He smiled when Janice cried with delight over Melanie and buried his own grief, as he filled in the woman he still thought of as his sister, with the details of the last two weeks.

He was strangely reluctant to talk about Lauren, except to say that she was a friend who had helped him out. Janice looked at him as if she wanted to urge him to say more, but then thought better of it.

Over the next week, Rick went to work as usual, leaving Melanie with Janice and Barry. It gave them a chance to know her better and to get used to her routine.

It was after an early dinner on the following Friday night that Rick finally broached the subject of when they intended to return to New York with the child. He was dreading the moment, but he knew the sooner they went, the sooner he could work out a way to get Lauren back. He loved her and he was positive she loved him in return. He had to convince her his love surpassed anything else, including any regret at not being able to give her a child.

And he knew he couldn't hide from that disappointment. Of course he had wanted children of his own, but the simple fact was, he wanted Lauren more. There were plenty of children in the world without parents to love them. It would be no hardship to adopt if Lauren were willing.

His gut clenched with longing every time he thought about her, which was often, and he wondered at his own self-control. All week, he had barely restrained himself from racing to her house and pouring his heart out. It was fear that kept him away, fear of further rejection. Although the excuse he gave himself was that she needed time to herself.

"Janice, have you given some thought about when you'll be returning home with Melanie?"

He felt his heart contract with the anticipated loss, but he quickly reassured himself that he could visit Melanie as often as he liked. Perhaps he could even move to New York. He wondered briefly if Lauren had ever been there.

Janice looked at her husband for guidance.

"We... er, were thinking of leaving the day after tomorrow," Barry answered for her. "That's the date on our return ticket. We could change it, but Janice would like to get back to Kathleen. And the other kids, for that matter."

Rick's stomach dropped like a stone. "Yes, I do see –"

"But we're not taking Melanie with us," Janice announced.

Rick stared at her. The silence was deafening. Rick tried to absorb Janice's words, but he couldn't seem to understand their meaning. "Pardon me?"

Janice left her chair and went to sit next to Rick on the sofa. "You know about our situation... with Kathleen and everything. Barry and I aren't getting any younger —"

"You're only forty-five," Rick burst out. He felt cold. Surely Janice wasn't going to suggest they foster Melanie out!

"I know, but we've got Billy and Jacquie at school. They're only twelve and fourteen. Then there's Patricia. She's in her first year of college and still living at home. Another baby on top of that would be... difficult."

"To say the least," said Barry gruffly.

"I can't believe I'm hearing this! You aren't going to abandon Melanie... are you?"

Janice placed her hand on Rick's arm and squeezed. "No, Richard. Of course we're not." Her voice held a surprising amount of calm. Even amongst his confused thoughts he registered that much.

"Barry and I have talked about this long and hard," she continued when he just looked at her in bewilderment. "We've noticed how you are with Melanie. You're a natural father, Richard. We think Melanie should stay with you."

Rick was speechless. He could see the sense in Janice's argument. Hell, who wouldn't think enough was enough after five children, one of them a prospective single mother, but... He glanced up at Barry. The other man's face gave nothing away, but at that moment Rick felt he understood.

Janice was giving the child to him. She knew how much he loved Melanie; maybe she had even guessed how deeply his feelings ran for Lauren.

"Thank you," he said finally, huskily.

Janice's eyes were filled with tears. "There's nothing to thank me for. It's us who should thank you."

Rick put his arm around Janice. She leant into his shoulder. "You're the best brother a sister could ever have," she whispered brokenly.

He patted her hair. A surge of pure joy enveloped his body and he had to dampen down his emotions in light of how Janice must be feeling. "Don't cry. Please. It's not as if you're giving her up. Not really. She's still part of your family... our family. But if you want to change your mind, it's not too late."

Janice lifted her tear-soaked eyes to Rick. She gave him a watery smile. "No. I won't change my mind. I've been thinking about it all week. Even before that. Melanie should be with you. I have my children and Melanie will still be my niece. You're right about that. She'll come to visit so often, our place will be a second home to her."

He smiled. "Exactly. So why are you crying?"

"I don't know." She brushed at her wet cheeks and tested a tremulous smile. "I'm just so happy everything has worked out. I know it's what Kelsey and Carl would have wanted."

Rick looked over at Barry. "What do you think about all this?"

"I want what's best for Janice, of course, but I knew all along another baby was more than she could cope with. Of course Kathleen's situation hasn't helped matters."

"No, I guess not," said Rick quietly, not wanting to start the other man on a subject which was likely to bring fresh tears from Janice.

Janice wiped her eyes. "Richard, I know this is the best solution for everyone. And I know Kelsey would approve."

Rick nodded. "Yes," he said. "I believe she would. And I'll do my best to be the best father Melanie could hope for." He paused, "I only hope I can convince Lauren she would be the best mother."

The seven days since she had left Rick's house were the worst of Lauren's life. Every time the phone rang, she was terrified it was Rick and then, when it wasn't, she felt deflated. She gave herself a number of stern lectures about the futility of her yearning but it was no use. The pain refused to go away. Eventually, she convinced herself that she just needed time to get over Rick. Life would go on.

In the meantime, she ached to know how Melanie was doing and whether Janice was coping with the baby on top of her own problems. Perhaps everything had settled down with Kathleen and life was looking up for all of them. Lauren's state of mind alternated between anxiety, that Janice couldn't look after Melanie properly, and then fell to the pits of depression, when she reassured herself that she, Lauren, wasn't essential to Melanie's well-being.

On Monday, she called her boss at the department store to see about getting her old job back. She knew it was unlikely as she'd been away for several months, but she decided to try before looking elsewhere. As it turned out, one of Lauren's colleagues was taking six months off to go overseas. Her employers were happy to offer Lauren the position. Unfortunately she had another two weeks to wait before the girl actually left.

It gave her far too much time to think about Rick and Melanie and how much she so desperately missed them.

Friday came around again, and with it, Brian and his usual chess game with her father. She contemplated calling up Tricia to see whether her friend would like to go out, but she had already had coffee with her earlier in the week and it was obvious Tricia was deep into a new relationship. She knew Tricia would cancel any plans for the evening to support her friend but, loath to put anyone out, she decided to stay home.

She had also had a long talk with her father during that week. They had chatted far into the night and had sorted out a lot of old hurts. She knew her father loved her, understood that his inability to cope with the grief over his wife's death had turned him into the hard man of her teenage years.

She also discussed her feelings for Rick and Brian. He listened sympathetically, but advised what she already knew; that only she could decide whether she loved Brian enough to marry him.

Good advice, except that she knew now that she didn't

love Brian. Her feelings for him were a pale shadow of the powerful emotions that Rick evoked in her. Brian didn't stir her blood or make her heart pound the way Rick could. She knew she would never love anyone the way she loved Rick. Knowing that, shouldn't she take what was on offer from Brian and have some happiness in her life? Marriage to a man who loved her seemed a better prospect than a lifetime of loneliness.

She still hadn't made up her mind when Brian arrived promptly at seven on Friday night. She opened the door to his smiling face.

"Lauren! I'm so glad you saw sense and came home again."

Lauren swallowed her annoyance. She had almost forgotten how supercilious he could be. But she could overlook that, she supposed. She had deliberately not contacted him during the week to let him know she was home. She realized with some reluctance that she hadn't missed him at all.

"Hello Brian."

He leaned forward to kiss her; she quickly averted her head so that it was her cheek that received his eager lips.

"I hope you're ready to give me an answer tonight. I've been very patient," he added reproachfully.

"Yes. We can talk later. After dinner."

The meal was a strange affair. Lauren was subdued and tense, Brian nervous and talkative. Throughout dinner, Lauren's father looked from one to the other with a question in his eyes.

As soon as Lauren cleared the dinner plates, he declined dessert, declaring that he was going to the tavern. "To give you young ones some space," he explained sheepishly.

Lauren almost smiled at the relief in his eyes when she agreed it was a good idea.

She closed the front door after her father and walked slowly back to the living room where Brian had made himself comfortable on the sofa. She took a deep breath and pasted a smile on her face before reluctantly sitting down next to him.

"Alone at last," Brian said with a tense laugh.

"Brian, I —"

"Lauren, there's something I want to say first."

She tried to relax. She should have been relieved the inevitable was to be delayed a few minutes longer, but she could feel a headache coming on. Even now, she wasn't sure what her answer would be.

Brian picked up her hand and squeezed it. She resisted the urge to pull it back onto her lap.

"Lauren, I know you don't love me. I can see it in your eyes. No, let me finish. I don't mind. I love you enough for both of us and it doesn't matter about children. I'm not that keen on them anyway. I love you Lauren. Please marry me!"

Lauren stared into his face. He was so sincere and she believed he did love her. But was it enough? She thought about the alternative and opened her mouth to give her answer.

Into the expectant silence she heard Rick speak. *Believe in yourself and you can have whatever your heart desires.*

For a heart-stopping second she thought he was really in the room, but she quickly reassured herself that his warm, husky voice was only in her mind. She came to an immediate decision.

"Brian... I'm sorry. I can't."

Brian frowned. "It's that Rick fellow, isn't it?"

She said nothing.

"I knew it! That huge house and that fancy car. He's

turned your head. Well, I can't promise all that, but I can promise to love you." Some of the harshness disappeared from his face. "I do love you, Lauren. Are you still angry with me about the baby? Is that it?"

Lauren sighed. She felt as if a great weight had been lifted from her shoulders now that she had finally made up her mind. She knew she had made the right decision. "No, Brian. It has nothing to do with the miscarriage, and it's not Rick. I just don't love you. It's as simple as that. I'm sorry."

"I know you don't love me, but it doesn't matter. Please Lauren..."

"But it does matter. To me," she said quietly.

"That's your final answer?"

"Yes. I'm afraid so."

He stared at her for several seconds before standing. "I guess I'd better be off then."

She followed him to the front door. "I'm sorry, Brian," she said again. Despite knowing she'd done the right thing, she hadn't wanted to hurt him.

As he opened the door, he turned. "Do you think your father will still want to play chess on Friday night's?"

She smiled to herself. "I'm sure he will."

He visibly brightened. "That's good. He's a good guy."

"Yes. Yes, he is."

Brian looked uncomfortable. "Well, it's goodbye then," he said gruffly.

"Goodbye, Brian." She kissed him on the cheek.

"I hope you find what you're looking for," he said before stepping outside.

Lauren watched him walk down the path then closed the door. She leaned back against the hard wood and sighed. She felt a strange mixture of relief and sadness. "The end of a chapter," she murmured to herself.

She walked slowly back to the living room and looked around. A kind of peace had settled. She felt her mother's presence keenly. She blinked away tears and tried to smile. "I miss you, Mom," she said. "But I know you would have agreed with me." She picked up a photo from the piano. It was one of the last ones ever taken of her mother. She stared at it for a long time, until the peel of the doorbell broke into her reverie.

"Dad must have forgotten his key."

She replaced the photo and walked quickly to the front door. "Who is it?" she called.

"Rick," came the muffled reply.

She wrenched the door open. "Rick!" she gasped before she could think of displaying a more circumspect demeanor.

He stood under the porch light. Lauren's heart shifted in her chest, an urgent wave of longing swamped her body.

Rick stared at Lauren. Was it really only a week since he had seen her? Somehow she seemed more beautiful. Sadder, but with an ethereal loveliness that made him want to take her into his arms and protect her from life.

"Rick," she said politely. "What can I do for you?"

He almost smiled at the way she pulled herself together. The expression on her face when she'd opened the door had told him everything he wanted to know. She had no hope of recovering ground now. However, she hadn't looked at Melanie once. The fight within to prevent her eyes from wandering was almost tangible.

"Hi," he smiled. "How are you?"

He almost cringed at his inane words, but he was too busy drinking in the faint musk of her perfume to care if he sounded like a total fool.

"Why are you here?"

"You forgot something," he said gravely.

"Oh. You could have called. Dad would have gone over to pick it up."

He grinned. "I think Melanie might object to being referred to as a piece of luggage."

He watched her eyes shift to the baby. Finding herself the center of attention at last, Melanie leant forward, her arms outstretched. "Ma, ma," she gurgled.

Lauren's face crumpled. "Rick, is this some sort of cruel joke?"

"Oh, honey, no! We wanted to surprise you. We've got some good news."

She blinked in bewilderment. Melanie was bouncing in Rick's arms, still reaching for Lauren, but she stoically refused to take the child.

"What is it?"

"Can I come in?"

She looked hunted. "I don't..."

"Please."

"No! Please say what you have to say and go."

He sighed. "It's about Melanie."

"Is there something wrong?" She looked at Melanie with concern in her eyes.

"No, Mel's fine. It's just that Janice and Barry aren't going to accept custody of her."

"But — surely you won't give her up to strangers!" she yelped in alarm.

"No, no. Of course not," he said quickly. "As a matter of fact, I'm going to take over as her legal guardian."

When Lauren didn't immediately react he continued. "I'm going to keep her and I want you to marry me," he said in a rush. "Please, Lauren, say you will. I love you so much. I... think you love me too." He looked uncertain. "Lauren..." His voice was unusually husky. "You didn't really mean it when you said you didn't love me, did you?"

Lauren tried to speak, but the constriction in her throat prevented it. She could only shake her head.

"Is that a yes?" he asked tentatively.

She laughed and threw her arms around him. Melanie giggled as she was squashed between them. "I said yes, you funny man." She clung to him and buried her face in his neck. "Oh, Rick. I do love you! I never stopped loving you. She pulled away. "I've been so wrong," she said softly. "I should never have run away. I just didn't think it was fair. You want children... And all those awful things I said. Can you forgive me?"

"Oh, Lauren!" groaned Rick before he swept her back into his arms. "Of course I forgive you! And it doesn't matter about children. We'll have Melanie and we can adopt more if you want or, if you don't, it doesn't matter. I just can't bear to live without you. We'll be a family and –" He didn't relax his tight grasp. "Just say you'll marry me. Please, my darling. Say yes!"

She laughed even as tears poured down her face. "Yes, yes, yes!"

He shifted Melanie to his other hip and stroked Lauren's cheek softly. "Lauren, I tried to tell you. You mean more to me than any child I may or may not have. I could never have been happy without you, no matter what else happened in my life. I love you with all my heart. I would go to the ends of the earth and back for you. Can you understand that?"

She swiped at the tears running down her face. "Yes, I can understand because I feel the same way."

Suddenly Melanie leapt forward out of Rick's arms and Lauren caught her, laughing. "I think she got bored with our conversation."

He chuckled. "No. She just knew whose arms she'd rather be in."

"Ma, ma," said Melanie again.

Fresh tears spurted from Lauren's eyes. "I'm so happy," she said through her tears.

"Am I interrupting something?"

"Dad! Oh, Dad, this is Rick and he's asked me to marry him. I've said yes."

"Thank goodness for that," he said. "I thought for a moment I'd have to escort him off the premises for upsetting my little girl. In my younger days that mightn't have been a problem, but now..."

Lauren laughed through her watery eyes. "Oh, Dad!"

"And who is this?" he asked as he looked at Melanie.

"This is Melanie. Rick's going to keep her and that means I'll be her mother." Her bottom lip trembled as she was overcome with emotion all over again.

"Looks like you two need to do some serious talking. How about I take this little girl inside?"

"I don't know if she'll go to a stranger," said Rick.

Lauren's father ignored Rick's hesitation and lifted Melanie out of Lauren's arms. Melanie stared at him in bewilderment as he looked into her face with a suspicious misting in his eyes.

"Aren't you a beautiful little lady," he said gruffly.

Melanie broke into a broad grin.

"What did I tell you?" he said smugly before turning away. "Why don't you two have a seat in the living room while Melanie and I organize coffee."

"Thanks Dad," Lauren smiled before leading Rick through to the living room.

She watched wistfully as her father walked away with Melanie in his arms. "He's acting like a grandfather already." She smiled before turning back to Rick.

Rick pulled her into his arms and held her tight. Neither spoke as they clung to each other. Finally, he withdrew enough to look into her face. "Did you really mean it? Do you really love me?"

She touched the moisture at the corner of his eyes. "Don't ever doubt it," she smiled before moving back into the comfort and warmth of his arms.

"Oh, I nearly forgot," Rick said as he eased himself gently away from her and reached into his pocket. He extracted a small jeweler's box of black velvet and held it out for her.

She stared at it for two full seconds before taking it and easing the lid open. She gasped. Nestled in more black velvet was a brilliant emerald and diamond engagement ring.

"Oh... Rick!" she breathed. "It's gorgeous."

"The emerald is the exact color of your eyes. I couldn't resist it," he smiled. He lifted the ring from its velvet bed and slipped it on her finger. The diamonds surrounding the clear green of the emerald flashed under the light.

She continued to stare at the ring, totally lost for words. Rick tipped up her chin with his finger and kissed her lightly on the lips. "I don't believe in long engagements," he murmured.

"Good. Neither do I."

"How does next week sound?"

She lifted her head and looked into his eyes. They were dark pools, almost black and glittering with strong emotion. "I'd marry you tonight if it could be arranged," she whispered.

He chuckled. "I doubt that's possible, but we could start a new trend."

She frowned in question.

"We could have the honeymoon before the wedding."

She smiled seductively. "Now that does have possibilities."

"My darling, cheeky minx. Hold that thought!"

Also available this month from

Mitchell's Valley

Amy Gallow

In Andrew Mitchell, Cynthia Sheldon discovers a man who would defy every obstacle, even death, to save his beloved Mitchell's Valley. When he rescues her from a blizzard and leaves before she can thank him, she pursues this gallant enigma across the mountain valleys, to the Mitchell ranch itself. In the process, she finds a horseman in the mold of a Texas legend, a mining engineer with a lust for gold, and a message from across the bridge of time. To find love, she must unravel Andrew Mitchell's mystery, face death itself and overcome her fear of loneliness.